Inked Passions

A Love Struck Bad Boys Romance

By Amber Burns

Published by Scarlet Lantern Publishing

1

Cade looked at his empty glass, foam nestled in the bottom. Lou Lou's catered to the rough and tumbler type. Located off a dirt road, but still close enough to the city to see the lights, most bikers knew where the best craft brew was. Cade stretched his arm to signal to the bartender he wanted a refill. A small burn from his newest ink rubbed against the protective gauze on his right bicep, reminding him he had just left the parlor a few hours ago. His arms were covered in full sleeves, ink in different colors and custom art covered from his knuckles to his shoulder. A large red dragon snaked up his left arm. Tribal tattoos in black and vibrant greens and reds spread from his right bicep to his chest. His latest tattoo, the one that still burned, was dedicated to his parents.

When Cade was four his parent's overdosed in front of him. He could still see the filthy apartment they lived in, and his parents sitting on an old lumpy brown couch, needles in their arms and vacant stares in their eyes. The image of that day forever burned into his memory. Sure, he may occasionally enjoy a puff off a bowl, but anything requiring a needle was out of the question. It's a wonder he ever had his first tattoo, but after the first he was addicted. Something he must have taken away from his parents.

After his parents died, Cade lived with his aunt for a few years, but she was always away on business trips. When he was seven, word got out that he was abandoned all day, and before too long he was in the system. He floated in and out of foster homes until he turned seventeen, when he ran away from his abusive foster father. Memories flowed into his mind like the smoke that filled his nostrils from the bar customers. Smoky, dark and twisted memories invaded his brain. The bartender replaced his empty glass with a new one full of the delicious pale ale from their tap. The foam head sloshed over and spilled from the cup's rim when she sat it down.

"Here you go sugar, anything else I can get ya'?" A husky voice brought him back to his senses.

The little black haired beauty in front of him was new. She wore a red button up shirt, cut very low, as low as she could, and tied in a knot to show off her thin waist. Her large round breasts practically spilled out of the top. She batted hre big green eyes at Cade and leaned a little too close to emphasize her exposed flesh, and intentions. He wondered how she even got into the skin tight blue jean shorts that left nothing to the imagination. Any other day, he would have taken her up on the seductive offer, but today was the thirtieth anniversary of his parent's death; and he was not in the mood.

"Just the beer," Cade replied coldly.

She shrugged and moved down the line of paying customers, shoving her breasts in their face. Cade pulled his attention from the bartender and looked in the mirror above the bar. His dark brown hair was a little shaggy but he kept it brushed back. Cade ran his hand through his scruffy brown beard and stared into his own sad green eyes. He sat for a while, taking his time enjoying the beer. When he reached the bottom of the glass again, he paid a different bartender and collected his jacket to leave. Outside, he could see his warm breath against the cold. He took out his lighter and lit a cigarette.

"No, get off!" A panicked voice screeched from the shadows behind the bar.

Cade moved quickly towards the voice that was now muffled and pleading. Around the shadowed corner he saw the black-haired bartender fighting to get away from one of the other customers, he recognized her attacker, Jimmy Osbourne.

"Get off the lady Jimmy." He took a drag from his cigarette.

"Mind you own damn business Cade." He turned back to trying to grope the bartender.

Cade sighed and flicked his smoke to the side. Not willing to give a second chance, or warning, Cade stepped right up to Jimmy and ripped him away from the woman. The sharp smell of hard liquor and smoke seeped from Jimmy's pores. Jimmy swung out at Cade, but his aim was off due to complete drunken stupidity. Cade clenched his fist and punched Jimmy in the left eye, taking Jimmy down in one blow. His drunken stupor and the shock of the blow knocking him out almost immediately.

"Get inside and do not come out with any of these men again."

The girl was sobbing, but she collected herself and rushed to him. Before he knew it, she planted a big kiss on his lips. Tears still streaming down her face, makeup running, she turned and ran into the bar.

Women are so strange. She was nearly raped and she kisses a complete stranger.

He shook his head and looked at Jimmy. *Serves him right.* Cade hooked an arm under the unconscious man and drug his body around to the front of the bar. Then Cade brushed off his hands and made his way to his jet-black motorcycle at the back of the lineup of bikes. Pushing off from the gravel around Lou Lou's, the engine from his bike purring between his legs, Cade made his way back to his apartment in the city.

His apartment sat above a night club with music flowing out into the streets. Many businesses in the square rented out the spaces above to willing occupants. Tonight, like every Friday evening, a big screen and projector were prepared to cast old black and white classic. People filled the fold out chairs provided and many brought their own blankets to scatter around and watch the film.

Cade avoided the couples strewn out across the square and punched in the code to access his upstairs apartment. Once in his apartment, he hung his leather coat on the back of a chair and grabbed another beer from his fridge. Popping off the bottle cap, he took a sip of the cool liquid and looked at his counter. Months of mail piled up in the corner, but the fancy envelope he had been avoiding poked out from the middle. He set his beer down and pulled the silver and teal envelope from the stack.

Inside, a picture of his best friend Tommy and his bride to be, Heather, smiled back at him. When Cade first hit the streets, he was alone but he soon made a friend for life. When Cade first saw Tommy, he was nothing but pale skin and bones. His eyes were hallowed out and his skin was dry with track marks racing up his arms. Tommy was strung out on intravenous drugs, like Cade's parents had overdosed on, and Cade helped him find the courage to seek help for his addiction. Together they went to the local rehab center, and Tommy started treatments. The first few weeks were torturous and slow, but after a few months of weaning off the drugs, Tommy's health began to improve.

Heather was a nurse at the rehab center and after Tommy was finally off his treatments and even working he found the nerve to ask her out. At first she was hesitant to date a past patient, but they soon hit it off and after a few months, Tommy moved in with her. They had dated for many years now and it was inevitable that Tommy would eventually marry her. Tommy knew how much Cade hated weddings, yet Cade was staring down at the letter where Tommy asked him to be his best man. He would do it of course. Tommy was his family after all.

Their wedding was only two weeks away, and Cade still needed to be fitted for his tux. He picked up the phone and gave Tommy a call.

"Hey man, yea, well you know, I have been pretty busy with the shop," Cade explained, trying to excuse his procrastination.

He listened as Tommy filled him in on the last few weeks. Where Cade had picked Tommy up and sobered him up, Heather had motivated him to finish school and improve himself professionally. Nobody would believe that their smooth-talking news anchor with the salt and pepper hair and filled in cheeks, ever spent time on the streets.

"Well, I am free tomorrow for a fitting," Cade relented. "Ok, see you then."

With the next day squared away, Cade got off the phone and went to take a quick shower. Once the days stress had melted under the heat of the hot water, Cade stepped out from the steamy mess and looked in the mirror. His new tattoo was a pair of praying hands with a rosary wrapped around them. A date rested beneath the prayer beads, his parent's death. Drying himself off with a towel, he checked his phone for any messages and finding none he climbed into bed naked. His Egyptian cotton sheets were the softest he could find and he quickly drifted off to sleep between them.

When Cade pulled his bike up to the curb of the formal wear store, he was surprised to find Heather with Tommy. He sighed. He liked Heather, but he had hoped they would catch a beer after and he knew that she would not be interested in such an outing in the middle of the day.

"Hey Cade." She smiled at him, her red hair waving in the cool breeze.

He always thought that Heather was beautiful and perfect for Tommy. Their relationship was the longest lasting one Cade had ever witnessed. He gave her a hug and then punched Tommy on the arm.

"Took you long enough," Tommy complained with a smile.

Cade returned his smile as the trio moved into the building. After forty torturous minutes of measuring every inch of Cade's body, a tuxedo was on order and would be ready in just a few days. Then they moved to shoes and other various accoutrements. When they left, Tommy pulled his friend to the side and handed him two small black boxes. One ring sat in each box. Tommy's was a simple band of silver tungsten, a single black strip of onyx rand down the center. Heather's was a delicate white gold band with three diamonds in a row, twinkling as he tilted the box to look at the gemstones.

He patted Tommy on the shoulder as if to say *good job*, and tucked them away in his coat pocket for safe keeping.

"Look, I know you hate weddings and any formal events, but thank you man." Tommy hugged Cade.

"No worries, you and Heather are family." Cade smacked Tommy on the back and they stepped apart to clasp hands.

"See you at O'Claire's on Friday night before the wedding." Tommy grinned his lopsided smile at Cade. As long as there was beer involved, Cade could stomach any bachelor party.

"Sure. See ya then."

They each went their separate ways. Tommy caught up to Heather and wrapped his arm around her shoulder as the made their way down the sidewalk. Cade returned to his bike and thought he should go home and work on a few of the commissioned pieces of ink he had.

Back at his apartment, he took out the design requests for his scheduled appointments and began drawing. One girl wanted a dragon wrapped around her thigh, its claws digging into her flesh. Another had a portrait of a baby she wanted on her arm. She had not specified if this baby had passed away or was still living, but Cade always enjoyed drawing portraits, no matter the story behind them. His last request for the week, involved a unicorn and a beer bottle, he was still perplexed at the request.

Once again, he took his shower, looked into the mirror and climbed naked into bed. He looked up at his ceiling fan as it slowly rotated around and around. Tomorrow was Sunday and he had to get the shop ready for the upcoming events. They did fundraisers every year. Patrons could come get a tattoo and donate so much of their proceeds to any of the various foundations of their wishes. They almost always had around ten charities to choose from. Labeled buckets showed the patrons who and what they were donating to.

Not able to sleep, Cade threw back the covers and quickly dressed. He grabbed his leather jacket and made his ways downstairs. It wasn't too late to get in a good fight. For those that were aware of it, an underground fighting ring was both a source of entertainment and a chance to earn a little cash. Weapons were not allowed in the ring, but it wasn't unheard of for someone to sneak in smaller easily concealed weapons. Cade straddled his bike and started the engine. 1800cc's rumbling beneath him. The sensation sending a thrill through him, that feeling never got old.

2

———

Dim city lights glowed around him and the streets were pretty quiet this hour. Riding at night was one of Cade's favorite things to do. He turned down a dark alley and parked behind a row of bikes. Many came to the ring on foot, few by car, but most by bike. Cade walked past a smelly overflowing dumpster. The sour smell of refuse invaded his nostrils and he covered his nose and mouth while heading for the unlit door.

Inside, people were jeering and applauding. Smoke and liquor permeated the air and Cade happily breathed it in. He walked down the steps that led into the establishment and headed for the bar. Surprisingly, he only recognized one name on the board as he added his own and paid the fee. It had been a few months since his last fight, but he was shocked more regulars weren't listed. A tap released its cool contents into a clean glass behind the bar, and Cade looked at it longingly. He didn't want to drink before a fight, but he was looking forward to a celebration beer after he knocked out his opponent.

"Hey Cade, how are you buddy?" A deep voice rumbled behind him as a large hand slapped him on the shoulder.

Cade turned and clasped hands with the giant. "Tank", or Larry if so privileged to know, had a growth disorder. His large towering form was frightening to most people, but Cade never treated him any different and they soon bonded over a pack of menthol's and whiskey.

"Tank, you handsome devil, how has business been?"

Tank was also the owner of this illegal establishment.

"Booming actually, after your ugly face left!"

He smiled, his large lips and teeth spanning the entire width of his face. Several teeth were missing and his large brown eyes had shadows around them. He looked tired to Cade but maybe that had something to do with his condition. Cade turned to the fight and saw he would be up in two rounds.

"The shop has kept me pretty busy. You should really come by for a tattoo Tank." Cade smiled and Tank shook his head.

"Always trying to stick me with your needles, oh that is right, your "pens". Bah! No, I will not allow you to torture me like that."

Cade had learned that Tank was afraid of all needles, which was a humorous concept to him. The man was so large, but he always avoided the topic of tattoos and piercings. They watched the fight in silence. Two young men, shirtless, walked circles around each other. Each watching the other for their next move, then one lunged, but it was a mistake. As he lunged, the other had prepared for this and slammed his fist in the side of the advancing man's head. The crowd erupted and the winner stood proud, sweat gleaming off his chest.

When the next fight ended abruptly, Cade turned to Tank.

"Well, wish me luck." He smiled, patted Tank on his large arm and strode towards the ring.

Cade stripped his jacket and crisp white shirt and placed them on a chair against the wall. He stretched his arms to release the tension that had built up between his shoulder blades and rolled his neck side to side, loosening up for the fight. Stepping into the ring, he heard a few shouts of his name. At least the crowd was still full of regulars that knew him and probably his impressive record.

Turning back he saw who he would be up against and smiled. The boy looked as if he was barely eighteen.

His skin was pale with a few tattoos running the length of one arm. His head was shaved, except for a strip down the center, which Cade assumed he was working on bringing back the mohawk style. His septum was pierced with a large curved bar hanging almost to his lips. He had also stripped off his shirt, revealing scars up and down his sides.

Cade walked towards him to extend his hand, a friendly hand shake before the fight, but the kid looked at his hand and spit to the side. The eyes that stared back at Cade were hard and unblinking, and they appeared almost completely black. There was something wrong with this kid, but Cade would just have to knock him around a bit and collect his earnings. Someone hit the bell to signify the fight had begun and the small pale skinned boy ran at Cade. Fists and feet rushed Cade in a flurry and he struggled to defend himself against the wild attack. He had not seen anything like this before.

Blocking the blows to his head and abdomen, Cade waited for an opening. He pushed the boy back and landed a quick punch to his side, but the young man kept swinging. Soon they hit the floor, tangled up with each other, sweat and blood mixing from their faces and knuckles. Cade's cheek was on fire and his lip was split but he felt good. He loved to let out his frustration in the ring. As they grappled, Cade thought he had the upper hand as he wrapped himself around the kids arm and began to apply pressure, but the kids arm went limp and he somehow snaked it out from Cade's grasp. They continued for a few minutes this way, exhausting one another, until finally Cade landed a punch in the kid's ribs.

Regretting the slight crunch he felt, Cade threw one more punch in the kids face and watched as he hit the floor of the ring. As always, the crowd erupted with excitement. Their fight was the most exciting one of the night. Cade walked over and bent down to make sure the kid was alright, but he pushed up from the floor as Cade neared and gripped his aching side. Flipping Cade a less than friendly finger, the boy walked away from the ring, still holding his side and slightly limping.

If he can walk, he should be ok, Cade hoped.

After the fight, Cade cleaned up in the restroom. He splashed cool water on his face and washed away the sweat and blood from his knuckles. He would need to ice those later. He looked at his face and was happy that his best friend's wedding was another week away. His face was red and a bruise began to blossom from the small wound on his cheek. Pulling his shirt back over his head, he felt an ache in his side as he reached above his head. Tomorrow was going to suck at the shop.

Tank waited for him at the bar with a cold draft beer and Cade was never more happy to see that ugly lopsided grin and the frothy beer in his oversized hands.

"As always, undefeated." Tank smiled and handed Cade his glass.

They clinked their cups and Cade took a large refreshing sip.

"I have missed this," Cade admitted as he looked back at the ring.

The lights had dimmed and most of the crowd had started to dwindle, the last fight satiated them till next time. Cade caught a glimpse of a bald head, thin strip of hair down the middle and a tatted up arm leaving with the crowd. Cade shook his head and finished his beer. Each of the winners had taken home a portion of the pot and now Cade stepped up to collect his. One hundred bucks wasn't much, but he pocketed it anyways and shook the coordinators hand.

"I am going to head out Tank, but I should be back in a couple of weeks."

"Stay out of trouble Cade, see you next time."

Stepping out into the dark alley, Cade quickly covered his nose to avoid the rancid smell of the dumpster. Out of the shadows, a figure jumped at Cade, surprising him. A street light glinted off something metallic that flashed out from the figure. A burning sensation ripped through Cade's side and a fist landed against his temple. Falling to the ground, pain blossomed from his side where his shirt felt wet against his skin. Cade spiraled into blackness.

3

He dreamt he was floating down a murky stream, twigs and branches grabbing and ripping at his clothing. A pinch in his hand slowly woke him from his dream. The twigs and branches were actually hands holding a pair of trauma shears to his red stained shirt. He discovered the pinching in his hand was an intravenous needle feeding him a slow saline drip as he was rushed down a brightly lit corridor. Something was pressing against his face, covering his mouth and nose.

In his blurred vision a blonde woman with bright blue eyes held the bag connected to the mask covering his face. He watched as her small hand squeezed the bag, providing him oxygen. His head throbbed from where he had been punched and his side felt like it was on fire as the busy hands worked to clean his wound. Those blue eyes stared down at him and for a brief moment he forgot about everything else, the pain, the noise, even the splitting headache. They pushed something else into his IV, and Cade's eyes rolled back into his head. Once again, he floated into the blackness.

When he finally woke, he blinked around the room and his eyes rested on Tommy passed out in a chair. Resting against him was Heather, reading a book and resting her head on Tommy's shoulder. A mounted television streamed the local news, and Cade looked at Tommy's clothes. He knew Tommy had skipped work to be with him. Looking around the room, he saw he was hooked up to a monitor, tracking his oxygen and blood pressure. Antiseptic and sanitizer filled the air and his senses. He knew he was in the hospital, but he couldn't figure out what had happened.

"What. What happened?" Cade whispered, his side hurting when he tried to sit up.

"Tommy, he's awake." Heather shook Tommy, who looked a little disoriented when he opened his tired eyes. Seeing that Cade's eyes were open, Tommy asked Heather to grab the nurse and he moved to Cade's side.

"Dude, you scared the shit out of us. You were stabbed in some alley. They aren't sure if it was a mugging attempt or what, because you still had your wallet and phone. You don't remember?" Tommy's brows were furrowed, concern etched across his face.

"I remember leaving the fight and a smelly dumpster, and I think there was someone waiting for me." His side hurt too much and Heather returned, followed by a nurse.

"Alright Mr. Winters, let's look at you." The nurse instructed as he walked around the hospital bed and checked the monitors. "Look's good. How do you feel?" The nurse started peeling back the gauze and protective layer over Cade's wound.

"Pretty shitty." Cade whispered.

The nurse smiled, as did Tommy and Heather.

"Humor is a good sign. Can I get you anything?"

"Water please."

The nurse took a cup from the cabinet and filled it with ice and water, then brought it close enough for Cade to reach.

"Thank you," Cade said and quickly took a few big gulps of the refreshing liquid.

"Alright, just press the nurse call button if you need anything." The nurse left the room and the three sat in silence for a moment.

"Well, I am glad you are okay buddy. I think we are going to head out for dinner, but we will be back tomorrow, sound good?"

Cade nodded his head to signal them to leave and he watched as they both left the room.

The next night he was discharged with wound care instructions, clean gauze, and antibiotics. Tommy and Heather had visited earlier in the day and he was thankful they were not there when he left the hospital. A cab brought him back to his apartment and he worried about his motorcycle. Not in any shape to physically check on it, he picked up his phone and messaged Tank. A moment later his phone lit up with a response, his bike was safe and Tank would keep it that way. At least that was one last thing he had to worry about.

Cade lounged around his apartment on that first day, ordering takeout and checking on his employees at the shop.

"Hey Cadence, how's everything going?"

"Going well boss," Cadence answered. "Alex rescheduled your appointments, and we have had several new customers. It's been a pretty steady couple of days, but we are doing fine."

Cade could hear the buzz of a tattoo gun in the background, mingling with a local music station from their stereo. He had only missed a few days of work, but was ready to get back to the shop.

"Well call me if you need anything," he instructed.

He hung up and stood up to go fix himself something to eat. His side was still very sore but the pain was slowly fading. Cade took out his laptop and checked his work and personal emails. A reminder to pick up his tux for Tommy's wedding flashed onto his screen. Looking at his phone, he thought about calling Tommy, but decided he wanted to get some fresh air.

It angered him that someone jumped him like a coward in the alley. His suspicions were on the scrawny, pale-skinned boy he fought. At least he survived and nothing major had been struck by the blade. Dressing was painful, but he managed. Cade walked on out and down the street towards Tanks. He needed his bike before doing anything.

"You look rough." Tank stood by Cade's bike.

"Thanks for keeping her safe." He patted his bike and climbed on. Stretching his arms to reach the handles, sent ripples of pain up and down his sides, but he was not about to leave without his ride.

Cade left the alley and Tank, and made his way to the formal wear store. After picking up his tux, he started to place his helmet on when he caught a glimpse of blonde hair out of the corner of his eyes. He stood frozen as his eyes traveled down that strangely familiar figure. His eyes moved to her face and rested on two clear blue eyes. A pair of naturally pink lips parted and she tucked a strand of blonde behind her ear. She wore a loose green top over a fitted pair of blue jeans, showing off her curvy hips. She was beautiful and carrying a large dry cleaning bag, satin and tulle poking out of the bottom of the bag. As she walked away carrying the large bag in one arm, phone to her ear, and coffee in the other hand, he wanted to run up and offer her help. Just then, a man opened a car door and she ducked inside. He watched as the man closed the door and walked back around to the driver's side.

"She has her own chauffeur?" He mused aloud.

Shaking his head, he finished putting on his helmet and prepared to leave. He knew her type, the wealthy snobbish type, it was for the best that he had not approached her.

Cade made it back to his apartment and climbed the stairs slowly. He realized he had not bought any groceries, but did not feel like going back out so he ordered takeout once again. Sitting down on his couch, he turned on the television and searched for anything good to watch. His eyes grew heavy, and before he knew it, he was asleep. He was floating again, that same murky stream as before and those twigs and branches were now flowers and leaves. His body came to a stop and he sat up, there in the clearing of the woods, a woman was stretched out on a blanket. Her blonde hair and blue eyes watching him intensely, as he made his way over to her. Just as he was about to come up to her, a loud screech sounded out. Awaking suddenly, Cade jumped and wiped his face with his hand. The doorbell was ringing, signaling him food had arrived.

4

"So, a unicorn and a beer bottle?" Cade asked as he looked at his client. After taking a few days to recover, Cade had returned to his shop to clear out his growing client list.

"Yes, I want the unicorn on the beer bottle, it's my own label for when I start brewing."

His client was a young college graduate, who had decided recently he wanted to brew beer.

"What does it mean?" Cade asked.

"You mean, what does it signify." His client corrected as he stretched out his hands in a grand gesture. "Mythical Brews." Cade nodded his head and smiled. "You see, I will have a different mythical creature on each style. On the label, we will have the name, the mythical creature, and a short description that ties in the creature and the different notes and ingredients of the beer."

"Well, that is actually pretty cool man." Cade was genuinely impressed. He was skeptical at first, but now he was interested in trying this kid's beer.

"Yea. We hope to get our license and start right away."

"Well, remember me. If you like my work, I hope you will bring me a beer."

Cade smiled and began the process of making the outline. After about an hour, he sat back, wiping away the ink and beads of blood and looked over his work. It was beautiful. He cleaned and covered the tattoo and sent the young man on his way. After locking up shop, he checked the time. He had to get ready for Tommy's bachelor party.

His apartment was within walking distance of the shop, so he headed back to the apartment and showered quickly. He dressed and sprayed some cologne on ready to bar crawl with his best friend. He met Tommy and a few of the guys from the newsroom at the Terry's Pool Hall. After the first two rounds of beer and a few game of pool, they moved along. One of the guys asked if they wanted to smoke, so they stepped outside and each passed around a joint. Cade was feeling very relaxed and enjoying himself. They made their way on to the next two spots, but by the third they were all already feeling the effects of too much alcohol in such a short amount of time. The men were forced to admit that they weren't teens anymore. Soon Tommy's other bridal party members cleared out early, most already married with children.

"Let's get something greasy to eat," Tommy smiled at Cade.

"Sounds good."

They headed to the diner. After they downed some cheeseburgers and fries, they sat back, nursing coffees.

"Did you want to do anything else tonight?" Cade looked at Tommy, who rested his head on the back of the booth, eyes shut.

"I actually would like to stop in at Mercy's," Tommy said quickly as he opened his eyes and raised his eyebrows at Cade.

"You want to go to a strip club? So, the most cliché thing for a bachelor party?" Cade was in disbelief.

"Well, it sounds fun."

"Let's go then, this is your night dude."

When they arrived at the strip club, they entered to find several older men and some women sitting around in booths. Bare-chested ladies ran around serving drinks and a few were performing private shows in shadowed booths. Cade was the least interested of the pair in such an establishment. He believed women should be treated with more respect, but if this was where his best friend wanted to go for his bachelor's party, he would go with him. At least he could keep an eye on him and make sure Tommy didn't do anything he would regret.

"This is pretty lame," Tommy grunted.

Cade smirked and downed the shot he had ordered.

"Want to leave?" Cade asked, hoping Tommy would agree.

"Actually, I would."

Good thought Cade. He knew he could stop Tommy from acting a fool, but had hoped he wouldn't need to. Heather was such a nice girl and they had been together so long, it gave Cade hope.

"Let's get you home. You are getting married in the morning dude!" Cade slapped Tommy on the shoulder.

"Just as a heads up, the maid of honor, she is a little stuck up. She is an ER nurse at the hospital, and she is going to school on top of working forty or more hours. Her father is some wealthy tycoon, so she has inherited a fortune. I have always liked Cindy, but I just thought I should warn you, especially since you two will probably have to share a dance if Heather gets her way."

Tommy sighed and Cade nodded.

"Thanks, I will keep that in mind."

They stumbled in late and laughing. The morning would be rough, but they would just have to manage with water and strong coffee. Cade crashed into his bed, fully clothed with Tommy crashed on his couch.

Early morning light streamed in through his window and Cade covered his eyes to try and hide from the pain. His head throbbed. When he walked into the living room he found Tommy stretched out and snoring loudly. He shook the groom to be, but when that didn't work he gave Tommy a few pats on the cheek until he woke.

"What...what time is it?" He asked smacking his lips and pinching the bridge of his nose.

"Time for you run and get ready."

"Ok." He called a cab and within fifteen minutes he had left. Cade only had a few hours until the wedding, so he showered to hopefully wash away the stink of last night and help sober himself up a little faster. After the shower, he looked in the mirror at his long shaggy beard, and got to work trimming and cleaning it. Cade brushed back his hair and have himself one last appraisal before dressing in his tux and calling a cab. The wedding was being held at a winery a few miles down the road and in the country. Since Cade missed the rehearsal dinner, he had to arrive early to practice.

When Cade reached the winery, he was taken down a twisting dirt road, rows of vines with purple globes were nestled along the side. It was a beautiful setting for sure. He groaned at the absurdity of it all. At the top of the dirt road, a large pavilion and rows of tables dressed with white linens were strategically placed. Little strings of golden lights were hung around the pavilion and purple and blue flowers sat in vases on every table. To the side of the pavilion, an elaborate arch was erected and covered in flowers, sat in front of rows of fold out chairs that were separated by a runner. Cade felt as if he had just stepped into a live version of some wedding magazine clipping.

Spotting Tommy, Cade paid the cab driver and strode over to the groom who was welcoming a few early arrivals.

"Hey man, looks nice." He said, pointing at the set up.

"Thanks. Hey, we are going to run through this pretty quickly since you didn't make it to the rehearsal dinner." Tommy showed Cade where he would be standing behind him at the altar, and told him the line the pastor would say to signify it was time to hand him the rings. Cade listened and even practiced handing him the rings, not wanting to mess anything up on his best friend's special day. A violin started playing quietly in the background, the soft notes just barely audible.

Cade looked back at the winery's main building and saw the curtains rustle and satin disappear out of view. He was a little nervous about meeting this Cindy character. Tommy had warned him she was somewhat prude. His mind drifted to the beautiful blonde he saw outside the formal wear store. He usually noticed pretty women and forgot them quickly, but for some reason he couldn't shake the image of this one. She even had revisited his dreams since the one on the river bank. He felt a thrill of lust at the memory of those dreams, and quickly pushed it away. Lusting for women he didn't know made him feel lonely, and he did not want that.

The guests started pouring in and filling in the seats. That same violin from earlier, was now accompanied by a cello, their melody humming through the quiet conversations of family reuniting and new family acquaintances. Tommy had repaired his relationship with his parents over the years. He had been living on the streets by choice, and had run-away from home at a very young age. His parents had never quit searching for him, and one day, years after Heather and Cade had helped straighten him out, he found them and apologized for the missed years. They were thrilled to see their young son turn into such an intelligent and successful young man.

They had also adopted Cade in a way. He was always welcome at the family dinners and events, and had attended a few. He preferred to be alone though, it had never been a problem for him, until recently.

"Cade, you look absolutely handsome." Mrs. Lane gave him a kiss on his cheek and squeezed him in a warm embrace. "Need to eat though!" She said as she patted his stomach. She hadn't known about his injury, and he wasn't going to let her know his side throbbed from the hug. He just enjoyed her hug and caring nature.

"Yes, ma'am. I need to come over for some of the best cooking again soon." He smiled at her and kissed her forehead.

"Hey son, how is the business?" Mr. Lane hugged him and then held him out by the shoulders, love shining warm in his eyes. Tommy actually had a little brother, but he passed away in infancy, so Cade had sort of filled the role.

"Business is great. We have your charity on our list this year."

Mr. Lane patted him on the shoulder in approval and turned to collect his wife.

"Come on Martha, let's leave the lad to his work. Best man is a stressful position." He winked at him and they made their way to their seats in the front row.

Cade stood there holding his hands behind his back. Tommy motioned for him to join him and the other groomsman. Mrs. Lane appeared out of nowhere once again.

"Tommy, where is Cade's corsage and a kerchief?" She was fussing with Tommy's shoulders and furrowing her brow at Cade's tux. She reached into her purse and pulled out both a corsage and a kerchief. Tommy laughed and kissed her on the cheek.

"I knew you would have them mom."

She batted away his affections and set to work folding the kerchief into Cade's front pocket and pinning his corsage too. He felt a little silly having a small flower pinned to his top. She then started fussing with his messy brown hair, trying to slick it back for him and also brushing off his shoulders and straightening his tie.

"That will do."

She looked over the two of them, but didn't seem completely pleased. She then turned to the other three groomsmen, but didn't fuss over them the same way. Returning to her seat, they all let out a sigh of relief and their shoulder relaxed. The music grew very quiet for a moment and then completely silent. Everyone in the crowd grew very quiet and soft notes began again. Slowly, a little girl walked down the aisle, her hair tied back and curled and her hands wearing lace gloves. She tossed little flower petals and giggled as she made her way down the aisle.

Next the bridesmaids came walking in slowly. Three ladies in floor length purple dresses walked in followed by Heather who was stunning in her white lace wedding gown. Behind her, the maid of honor trailed her, holding onto her train. Cade felt his heart jump into his throat. That same beautiful blonde that had haunted his dreams and memories from the other day was holding the train. She was moving slowly, and a little awkwardly. Her blonde hair had been curled and pinned back, and the purple satin dress she wore hugged her waist tightly and slightly fanned out around her knees. He saw the cause of her awkward walk. She wore silver high heels shoes, and with each step, she moved gingerly down the aisle to avoid tripping while holding the train to keep the bride from falling as well. He smiled at her, she was pure beauty and her awkward step was adorable.

Once they were all in place, Cade realized he was staring at her when her icy blue eyes turned on his. Where had he seen those eyes before? He felt like he knew her from somewhere, but he wasn't sure where. He tried to pay attention to the words of the pastor so he wouldn't miss his que, but she was standing there holding the bride's bouquet and he was ready for their dance. When Tommy had first told him there would be a dance between him and the maid of honor, he was not thrilled. Now he couldn't shake the idea of holding her body close to his.

As Cade stood motionless and staring at Cindy, he didn't hear his cue.

"Cade, psst!" Tommy's head was turned so he could whisper over his shoulder.

"Oh, sorry, here." He quietly, but quickly produced the two rings and the ceremony continued without any further disruptions.

"I pronounce you man and wife. You may now kiss the bride." The husky voice of the pastor drifted into Cade's senses and Tommy dipped Heather into a romantic and deep kiss.

Everyone cheered and the music from the music began to crescendo. Tommy and Heather turned to their guests and faces full of joy, they walked hand in hand back down the aisle as Mr. and Mrs. Tommy Lane. Cade stepped up and hooked his arm with Cindy's, his heart racing when they touched for the first time. She turned her bright blue eyes on his and a spark of recognition flashed behind them. They both paused, almost causing a bridal party pile up but they quickly continued down the aisle after the newlyweds.

Each couple made their way to the pavilion and Cindy, to Cade's disappointment, let go of his arm and hurried over to wrap Heather in a big hug. Soon, the guests came pouring in to congratulate the newlyweds with hugs, kisses, and handshakes. One of the tables was covered in beautifully wrapped wedding gifts and cards. Each table was already set with dinner plates and silverware for the guests to help themselves to the various hot and cold foods at the buffet. Pewter platters and chafers sat in a row with labeled white cards and gold text indicating each item.

All of the wedding party was supposed to take pictures with the bride and groom before eating. The aroma of succulent roasted chicken, creamy mashed potatoes, and buttery fresh baked bread filled the pavilion. A large six tier wedding cake sat on a table by the groom's cake. Cade walked over to get a closer look at what Heather chose to represent Tommy with. It was a chocolate cake with rolled up newspapers and a news anchor microphone resting on top. He thought it was an excellent choice for Tommy.

As the professional photographer moved them around into different group and couple poses, Cade kept catching glimpses of Cindy. He noticed a few times she was also watching him. Every time their eyes met, a slight blush filled her cheeks. His heart would beat a little faster, and he just wanted to talk to her. When they were finally done, he made his way to her, but once again she took off after Heather. They all filed into the dining area and took their seats at the head table. Time for the speech. He had not actually prepared anything, just thought he would wing it. A microphone was handed over to him and for some reason, he was instantly nervous. He had never had stage fight, so this was an interesting experience for him.

"Many of you know that I came into Tommy's life many years ago. Not too long after that, he met a beautiful red-headed angel, Heather. She is truly a gem and over the years she has been by his side. Tommy, man, I love you like a brother and I have to say, that I am so glad Heather came along to start taking care of you, because whew was that pretty exhausting," all of the guests gave a slight chuckle at that. "Anyways, Heather, you have made Tommy one of the happiest fools and I love you like a sister. I wish the two of you many happy years together." With that he raised his glass and handed off the microphone. Cindy reached for the microphone and her warm honey voice reached Cade's ears for the first time.

"Heather, I have known you since nursing school and our first days as sisters in Kappa Phi. We pinned each other in our white uniforms and spent our first sleepless nights, eating pizza after finishing our first exhausting clinicals. When you met Tommy, I thought 'oh no, trouble walking.' I was wrong, he is the kindest and most thoughtful person. He has brought you soup when you were sick, flowers on every occasion, and always put you first. Tommy, thank you for making Heather the happiest woman and here's to many blissful years!" She raised her glass, and everyone cheered.

Next, Tommy grabbed the microphone.

"Thank you everyone that is here to celebrate with us, we would like to join you on the dance floor and at the buffet. Please, help yourself. I am going to go boogie with my beautiful bride for a few moments on the dance floor."

He dropped the microphone and the disc jockey started the dance music. They even had colorful lights start with the music and the bride and groom made their way to the center. The first few songs were pretty fast paced, but then a slow song came on. Cade saw Cindy with a plate of food back at the head table and he made his way to her.

"Hello, may I have this dance?" He smiled at her, spoon of mashed potatoes half way to her mouth. She blushed and set down the spoon. He was slightly embarrassed for interrupting her meal, but he was so nervous he couldn't even think straight.

"Uh, yes." She nodded and stood up to take his hand. Her hand was cool in his warm one, but he loved the feel of it.

They walked out to the edge of the dance floor, not wanting to interrupt the bride and groom. He placed his hands on her hips and she wrapped her arms around his neck. He was instantly reminded of his middle school days. Molly Edwards with braces and frizzy hair had asked him to the homecoming dance. Not interested in going, but also not wanting to hurt her feelings he agreed. He had no idea he was supposed to buy her a corsage, and he also had no rhythm. When she went in to kiss him, he was so nervous and accidentally scraped against her braces.

Despite the awkward night, for several days Molly pursued him after the dance and he even heard rumors she was telling everyone they were a couple. Finally, with a heart-shaped and obviously hand-made card in his locker, he knew he had to tell Molly they were not in fact a couple. She burst into tears and never spoke to him again. After middle school, Molly straightened her hair and had dumped the braces. She eventually became rather stuck up, and he was glad he did not entertain her fantasy that they were together.

He looked into those bright blue eyes that felt so familiar and he inched a little closer to her.

"You don't remember do you?" She asked, her soft voice shaking him out of his memories. He realized he daydreamed a lot, most of the time on his own memories.

"Huh?" He was puzzled by her question.

"I was the nurse on call in the ER that night, when you were brought in on a stretcher."

Cade stopped moving side to side for a second and he realized those blue eyes were the ones that were full of concern as he looked up on the stretcher. That small hand, the one that felt so soft in his own, was the hand that held the bag squeezing oxygen into him. That also meant she was also the hand that cut his shirt off to assess the damage.

"I guess I never got around to thanking you, so thank you." He smiled at her.

"You are welcome. We don't usually get to hear a thank you. So, I am Cindy, Cindy Watkins." She smiled as she officially introduced herself to him.

"I, uh, I am Cade Winters, nice to meet you Cindy."

As the slow song faded, another took its place. He pulled her a little closer and he breathed her in. Her hair smelled floral and minty and wanted to bury his face in the nape of her neck to see how the rest of her smelled. He felt himself growing hard as her body was so close to his, invading his senses. Not wanting to alarm her, he shifted so she wouldn't feel the bulge forming against the inside of his leg. He tried to shake himself from this carnal desire, but her warm scent and proximity was overwhelming. The song slowed and he stepped back.

"Do you care if I join you with food?" Cade asked.

"No, I mean, yes… let's eat."

They made their way back to the buffet and despite having a plate already sitting at the table, she awkwardly grabbed another plate and stood in line with him. He loved her quirky mannerisms. She was awkward in heels and clearly nervous around him. He hoped that meant she was as interested in him as he was her. They took their plates back to their seats and sat down. Neither actually taking bites, they kept stealing glances at one as their food grew cold.

"So, what do you do?" She asked him as she finally sliced into her roasted chicken and took a small bite.

"I own my own business actually. I am a tattoo artist and I own the shop on Main Street, Inked Dragon."

He also took a quick bite of food, hoping his profession wouldn't be a deal breaker. He had met women in the past who ran from the idea of a motorcycle riding, inked up, tattoo artist.

"Oh, that explains your arms and chest. Did you design any of those yourself?" Her blue eyes shown with genuine interest and so he continued to divulge.

"I actually designed the dragon on my left, but I have let many of my friends custom draw the other ones." Not realizing he was stroking his beard, he stopped and ran a hand through his hair.

"That is really awesome. I have always wanted a tattoo, but I have never known what I would want permanently on my body." She took another bite. He wanted on her body. He wanted all over her body.

"Well, you should come by some time and I can show you my book. I would be more than happy to sketch you something." He winced. He wasn't supposed to talk shop.

"That would be great, maybe next week?" She smiled at him again.

"Yea, definitely, any day. Uh, do you like coffee?" He hoped she would say yes, he would love to take her for a coffee date before she came by the shop. He wanted to ease her in so she wasn't intimidated when she met some of his pierced staff.

"I love coffee, are you kidding!?"

They chuckled.

"Well, I would love to meet you at Loco Joe's if you would like, maybe Tuesday? Would you be available for an afternoon coffee?"

"I should be done with my shift by noon. Here, let me give you my cell so you can call me."

He pulled out his phone and punched in the numbers as she read them. After they grew more comfortable in company and conversation, they finished their plates. They were so distracted that they didn't even see the bride and groom cut their cake or head straight towards them with two giant slices of red velvet.

"Here you go, lovebirds." Tommy smiled and turned to Heather, wrapping his arm around her waist, they made it back to their own table.

They both had a bite of their cake and when they were finished, he noticed Cindy had a lick of frosting on her cheek. He was tempted to wipe it away and have a taste of her sweet rosy lips. Instead she wiped her cheek and sipped her champagne. They continued to talk for what felt like hours, he learned a lot about the woman sitting in front of him and shared some about himself. Soon the guests had begun clearing out and Tommy and Heather once again approached them.

"Hey guys, time to wrap it up." They smiled and kissed each other, then hugged Cade and Cindy good night. Cindy looked at the time and then at Cade.

"So, you want to go grab a beer?" She asked him and he grew excited.

"Yes, I definitely would like a beer." They called a cab and rode in silence as the cab driver took them to a bar back in the city.

5

Cade paid the driver and rushed around to open Cindy's door. She smiled and together, they walked arm in arm inside the still bustling restaurant. They sat at the bar and Cade ordered himself a beer. Cindy ordered a glass of wine and they continued their talk.

"Well, one time, a little old couple came in for a gunshot to the butt. His wife had shot him, then brought him into the emergency room. When the police questioned her, she said 'well, I was tired of his lazy ass leaving laundry everywhere. I told em' if he din't get his act together, I would pop him in his ass, so I did.' It was the funniest and most bizarre thing, but her husband didn't want to press charges. He apologized for not listening to her."

Stacey tried to stifle her laughter as the story ended, but Cade's laugh drew out her own.

"Well, we once had a guy come into the shop with his girlfriend, they were barely eighteen. He wanted her face tattooed around his left nipple, and he wanted us to pierce the nipple. Somehow, he expected us to make his nipple look like a pierced septum to match his girlfriend. It was the strangest request, but we somehow managed it. He came back a few months later requesting a cover up since they had broken up. Later in the week that same girl brought another poor guy into the parlor wanting her face tattooed in another, far more disturbing location. We apologized but refused the service. She was furious, but I am pretty sure I saw them a few weeks later, leaving Inked Spirit. He was limping and she had a smug look on her face."

"Oh no! Did he come into your shop for a cover up too?" She took a sip of her wine and looked at him over the glass, her beautiful blues shining.

"Not yet, ha."

He took another sip of beer. For the first time, in a long time, he was truly enjoying the company of another. In the past, conversation dwindled quickly and most of the time his quests turned into one-time sexual encounters. This was different. Cindy was different. He wasn't sure what he was feeling, and he thought it was too soon to feel so attached to someone but he wanted to learn more. He also wanted to learn the curves of her body.

She stretched and let out a soft groan and he realized she was still wearing those terrible silver shoes and her bridesmaid dress. She had to be uncomfortable. She tipped back her glass and finished the red liquid. He also finished the last bit of beer and placed his empty frothy glass on the counter, waving to the bartender.

"Ready to get out of here?" He asked.

She nodded and he paid for their drinks. They were only a few blocks from his apartment, but he wasn't quite sure if she was actually ready for that or not.

"I live a few blocks away, would you like to come back for a drink or would you like me to call you a cab?" His heart skipped a beat as he waited for her response.

"Your place."

She wrapped her arms around herself, and he saw gooseflesh rise on her arms and shoulders. He took off his jacket and wrapped it around her. They started walking down the sidewalk and a few feet away, she stopped.

"Damn it," she cursed under breath and she slipped off the silver heels, preferring to walk barefoot than to keep walking awkwardly in those heels. He hooked and arm around hers and took her shoes in his other hand.

"Thank you," she whispered.

"You are welcome. Those shoes are killer, are your feet ok on this pavement?"

"Yes, I have worn nursing shoes for years, barefoot is the best, trust me. Besides, what were you going to do, pick me up and carry me away? My trusty steed?"

"If I needed to, yes."

Cade played it off as a joke, but he was serious. He did not want her to have to walk in pain. She just chuckled at his response. They arrived before long and he stopped and looked at her.

"This is it," Cade announced.

She smiled and looked up at the old brick building, vines growing up the side. The nightclub was alive with the sounds of music and they headed up the stairs. Once inside, she set down his coat and looked around his apartment. He wished he had spent some time cleaning it up, but he also didn't realize he would be bringing a woman back to it tonight. He rushed to the fridge and took out two bottles of beer, popping off the tops he handed one to her. She looked at it for a second and smiled.

"I love a good Indian Pale Ale."

She took a sip and moaned from the refreshing flavor. He was in love. A woman that could appreciate beer and talk about gunshot wounds was a woman for him. He had to get her on the back of his bike to see if she would like that too.

"One sec," Cade interjected as he walked over to his television and put on a music station for them to listen to. Then he cleaned off his coffee table and invited her to the couch beside him. She walked over and looked out at the town square before joining him.

"Such a beautiful view!" Cindy cooed.

"Yea, I lucked out with this spot. I guess most people are not a fan of the nightclub below, but that has never really bothered me. I actually find the music to be a little soothing sometimes."

He took another sip and watched her. Cindy had spotted his drawings on the coffee table and was bent forward picking through them. Having his work analyzed by anyone had always bothered him. Not that he was afraid of a critique, positive criticism was wonderful, but for some reason it had always irked him if someone looked at his art work before he was finished. When Cindy looked at it, he was feeling nervous but not perturbed. He wanted to know what she thought, but he wanted her to tell him without any prompting or questioning.

"These are amazing Cade. You could win competitions or even be on television like that one female tattoo artists that's really big. I can't think of her name right now, but yea, this is awesome!"

It thrilled him to hear her say that. He caught himself staring at her again. Her neck was long and exposed from her blonde hair being pinned back and her collar bones were inviting him to kiss and nibble along them. Her chest was rising with each breath and he caught a small glimpse of cleavage with each heave. He soaked in her whole body, small waist, wide hips and long legs. She was beautiful and he wanted to explore her.

She looked up at him and their eyes met. She set down his drawings and her half-consumed bottle of beer on his coffee table and unpinned her hair, letting the blonde curls cascade and rest on her shoulders. She bit her lip as she looked at him. His yearning had returned and a heat overwhelmed him as he grew hard at the sight of her. He moved closer to her and set his own beer next to hers. Turning to face her, he placed his hands under her chin.

"May I kiss you?" He asked.

His vision was slightly blurred with lust and she parted her lips and nodded. He leaned in and softly kissed her, first just tasting her lips. She inhaled and he felt her tremor as he took her mouth deeper, exploring her. She was intoxicating. He laid her back on his couch and planted soft butterfly kisses along her jaw, down her neck, and resting at her collar bone, he kissed and ran his tongue across her flesh. More gooseflesh rose, but not from the cool night air this time.

He could see her chest rising and even through the satin gown, he knew her nipples had grown erect and hard with desire. Each feather light kiss caused ripples and trembles from her arching body. She pressed her hips up towards him, teasing him with what was to come. He slipped a hand under her and began to unzip the lavender gown. He pulled it down below her waist, her round creamy breasts exposed. Two deliciously taut beads of flesh tempted his mouth and took one of them in and licked around as he cupped her other breast.

She moaned as he took turned taking each nipple in his mouth, playing with it as he moved it around his tongue and teeth. Then he kissed down her chest, to her belly button. Her skin was soft, each kiss she moaned and rocked those beautiful hips. He slipped the dress completely off of her body and moved to taste her hips, pulling the lacey pink underwear down and around her ankles, she was completely naked on his couch, hips rocking with wanton desire.

Between her legs was smooth skin, a perfect juicy mound of pink flesh, slick with her lust. He continued to plant kisses on her flesh as he made his way to that soft pink center. She continued to moan as he slowly licked her clitoris and spread her lips to explore her deeply. Her taste was sweet and her scent was clean and floral like her hair. He continued to explore her, her hand coming around to hold him in place at her center as she rocked her hips against him, wanting more. Her moaning and panting grew more frantic, and he slowly slipped a finger inside of her. The one finger was welcomed and squeezed tight, sending shudders through him. He wondered how he would fit, if she was this tight with just one finger.

She continued to rock against his hand as he licked her clit and continued to tease her with his finger. She gasped and cried out as she climaxed for him and he moaned, wanting to feel that sweet tightening and pulsing around his hard cock. He stood up and she laid there, sprawled out, wet and practically humming from the orgasm. He began to undress, but before he could take off his pants, she sat up and stopped his hands. She unbuttoned and unzipped his pants, pushing them down and he kicked them off.

Her eyes grew large as she saw the large bulge hidden by his boxers, and he pulled them down, his giant cock exposed to her. She gasped and then took his throbbing member in her hand. She squeezed, a little too hard, but her hands felt so good. She then licked his head with her pink tongue, slowly flicking her tongue in circles. That felt really good, he shuddered and she stopped. Setting back against the couch, she placed her hand on her stomach and looked up at him, her hips rocking again. Cade moved to take a condom from the drawer of his coffee table. After he was covered, he placed himself between her hips and kissed her deeply.

Parting her, he rested at her entrance for a second, feeling the heat from her radiating up against his erect head, he slowly entered her. She moaned and gasped as he stretched her with his first thrust. Her tight pussy squeezing him so tight, he didn't know how long he could last. He began thrusting and she wrapped her legs around him, taking him in as deep as he could go. He hit that back of her womb and felt her pulsing and throbbing. She arched her back and cried out as the ecstasy of orgasm washed over her again and she panted against his chest. He grabbed her hips and thrust harder, causing her to cry out with pleasure. She tightened around him and bucked her hips in his direction, not quite matching his pace, but sending ripples of pleasure through him until he finally lost himself inside of her.

He moaned and kissed her as he throbbed inside of her, still reeling from the orgasm, he just wanted to rest on her soft flesh, deep inside of her. He inhaled her scent and nibbled her ear. Out of breath and sweaty, he rolled away from her.

"Mmmm, I would like to do that again," she purred as she laid there naked and worn out on his couch.

Her legs twisted together with his and she stretched. He smiled and pinched her still hard nipple.

"Oh, I planned to," Cade mock threatened. "I just need a little break first, and some pizza."

She laughed at him and sat up. It was late, but he managed to find one pizza delivery still running. They each ate a few slices and snuggled up together. To Cade's dismay, round two did not happen. Cindy had drifted off to sleep on his shoulder, a soft and steady snore coming from her lips. He kissed her on her forehead and laid her down so her head rested on a pillow. Covering her with a blanket he made his way to his own bed.

By the morning, she had already cleared out. The blanket left neatly folded on top of the pillow on his couch. Cade immediately reached for his phone, but then stopped.

Since when did I feel the need to call a woman immediately after sleeping with her? Well, she had stayed the night, which was further than most women got.

Trying to distract himself, Cade left for work. All day, clients came in droves for tattoos and piercings. Many had to be rescheduled, but for those that just wanted simple flash art, Cade saw that they were inked. He checked his phone but no messages lit up his screen. He would give Cindy a few days and then call.

A few days passed and still no word from Cindy. After arriving outside for the afternoon shift at his shop, Cade leaned to the side, resting his bike against his leg and picked up his phone to call her.

"Hello?" She sounded out of breath.

"Hey, Cindy, it's Cade."

"Hey! I was wondering when you would call me."

"Oh, I thought you would have called or messaged and I didn't want to disturb you," Cade tried to excuse himself.

"Well, I might have, if I had your number."

Cade paused, realizing he had gotten her number, but she had not his. He shook his head at himself, cursing himself for not calling her sooner, but thankful she sounded upbeat about everything.

"I had a fantastic time the other night, and I do remember you mentioning coffee for tomorrow," a playful tone entered her voice.

"Yes, around noon," Cade confirmed. "If you are still up for it."

"Of Course, see you there."

When Cade entered the shop, he was surprised to see Tank in the lobby.

"Hey Tank, finally come for your tattoo?"

"You wish," the large man guffawed.

"What is going on buddy?"

"That kid with the pale skin you fought a few weeks back. He has been causing trouble at the club and asking around for you. I thought I would warn you."

"Thanks man."

Cade was wondering what that kid wanted. Cade had won the fight fairly and then been ambushed most likely by the kid and left to die from a stab wound in a dark alley. What the hell did the kid want? The thought of the stab wound made him gingerly touch his side. It had been healing quite nicely, but was still very sore to touch.

"Will we see you around the ring anytime soon? I think that kid wants a rematch," Tank asked.

"Well, I have been preoccupied lately, but I may come back in a few weeks. In the meantime, avoid that kid if you can."

Tank turned to leave, having to duck to walk through the door.

"And Tank, watch out for any illegal weapons on the kid in the ring."

Tank's eyebrows shot up and then eyed Cade's side. Tank had been the one to find Cade in the alley only moments after the attack and called 911. Tank stood for a moment, shook his head and walked on out and down the street.

Cade was lost in thought when his cell started to vibrate in his pocket. The screen lit up with a goofy picture of Tommy and Heather.

"Hello," Cade answered.

"Hey man! So, Heather and I want to come in and get tattoos, just wanted to check your schedule."

"I'll block of this afternoon, come on in."

"Awesome, see you soon."

This was the not the first time Cade had given Tommy a piece, but it would be his first time inking Heather. He wondered if they were going to have matching tattoos, or something more original.

When they strolled through the parlor doors, Cade hugged them both. Heather looked around his lobby. The walls were painted a deep red and the floors were wooden and they creaked with every step. Black leather couches sat against the wall, and the artist's work filled the binders for customers to flip through. Flash art decorated the walls, but the fun jobs were the custom ones. Cade sat down with them on the black leather couch to go over the details of what they wanted.

"Ok, so, we want wedding bands, but we also want another piece." Tommy was holding Heather's hand.

"Ok, where and what?"

Cade was jotting down notes of what they wanted. Their "wedding bands" would be simple black bars that wrapped around their ring fingers and they both wanted the wedding date inside the black bar in green. He was worried it would fade and he told them so, especially on their hands, but that he would do it.

Next they each wanted their own personal tattoos. Tommy had an idea involving an all seeing eye theme and Heather wanted a fairy with a pixie cut and torn up dress. It was an interesting sit down, but Cade looked forward to designing these for them. In the meantime, he had them follow him back so he could get to work with their wedding bands. Tommy, not a stranger to tattoos, didn't flinch. But when Heather sat down and Cade went to work, he saw that her right hand squeezed the arm rest so tight her knuckles were white.

They were both excited when their swollen, pink fingers were done. Cade just smiled at them and gave them instructions on proper after care.

"I will have these designs done by the end of the week and we can discuss any changes you may want to make." Cade was standing in the lobby with them. Heather nodded and headed out the door.

"Hey, so what's going on with you and Cindy?" Tommy had waited till Heather was gone to ask.

"Nothing, we had a really nice time after the wedding and we are going to go grab a cup of coffee tomorrow." Cade was trying to be nonchalant about it.

"Well, I am shocked, happy for you, but shocked." Tommy raised an eyebrow at Cade, he clearly wanted more information.

"Yea, I was pleasantly surprised too." Cade was the most shocked that he loved her. He didn't know how he could possibly love her after just one evening, but he knew he never wanted anyone else but Cindy.

"Don't worry about it Tommy, I am a grown man." He slapped Tommy on the shoulder and headed him for the door.

"I know, but you have been through so much and I just don't want to see you get hurt."

"I am thicker than that man, I will be ok."

Tommy shook his head. "Cindy is great, it is her family that are questionable."

"Well, you also warned me that Cindy would be a horrid bitch, but she was far from it."

"Ok, we will see you soon. Later."

Tommy turned and left, seeing that he wasn't going to win an argument involving Cade's love interest. It did bother him a little that Tommy was so concerned about his own love affairs. He found himself wondering about her family, but he wiped the thoughts from his mind. He needed to talk to Cindy before he drew any conclusions.

6

The next day, Cade threw on his leather jacket and ran down the stairs to jump on his bike. It was almost noon and he didn't want to be late. Speeding never ends well, and the blue lights that flashed behind him made him groan in frustration. He waited patiently for the cop to approach. It was Veronica. She loved to give him a hard time.

"Hey Cade. Where you headed in a hurry?" He looked at him over her glasses, her brown hair tied back in a neat bun.

"A very important date," he smiled his best charming smile at her, hoping his beard didn't ruin the effect.

"Yes, well important enough to be going fifteen miles over the speed limit?" She had one hand rest in a fist on her hip and the other holding her clipboard. "You know the drill, driver's license and registration."

He sighed and gave her the proper documentations. A few moments later she brought them back and handed him a pink slip that he already knew said he owed over a hundred bucks for his violation.

"Slow down motorcycle Cade," she winked at him and walked back to her car.

Cade looked at the number on the document. It wasn't a ticket, it was actually her phone number. She rolled past him with a smile and drove off down the street.

Since when did she have an interest in me?

Cade shrugged, he was not interested in pursuing anything with her or anyone else that wasn't Cindy. Seeing that Veronica was well down the road, he crumpled up the pink slip and tossed it into a trash can on the sidewalk.

Cade's heart thudded in his chest and he parked his bike, took off his helmet, and went inside Loco Joe's to find Cindy. He looked around the room and spotted her in a corner booth reading. She was wearing her blue scrubs and her hair was tied back. She was beautiful. He ordered a mug and paid, then joined her in the booth.

"Sorry I am late. You are beautiful," He quickly added and picked up her hand, kissing her cool skin.

She smiled, a light blush rising on her clean cheeks. She wasn't wearing any makeup that he could see and she was perfect.

"I am so tired, but I have been looking forward to this cup of coffee all night."

He did notice how sleepy her eyes looked and he felt a pang of guilt for inviting her to coffee after working a long shift.

"Rough night?"

"It was a steady night for sure, but I have had worse nights for sure."

She placed her hand on her shoulder and squeezed, pain stitching across her brow. He moved to sit beside her and had her turn towards the window. He began rubbing and squeezing her shoulders and back and she moaned. He felt her relax under his hands and he wrapped an arm around her, pulling her close to him. She looked up at him with those sleepy blue eyes and he bent down to kiss her. His heart raced with exhilaration.

"This is crazy." She said a moment after their lips left one another.

"What?"

"I feel so comfortable in your arms. I have never felt so safe with anyone."

Her eyes shined brightly at his and it took a lot of will power not to scoop her up and undress her on the spot. He ached to be inside of her again. He wanted to feel her raw, wet and tight around him. Feeling himself harden at the thoughts, he shook himself and kissed her lightly on the temple.

"I completely understand what you mean."

He sighed and sat back up to take a sip of his coffee. They spent the hour together, sharing details of work. He told her about Tommy and Heather's tattoos and she described a night of patients that weren't emergent flooding into the hospital. She yawned and stretched, their coffee cups cold and empty.

"You need to get home and rest, do you have a ride?"

"I usually take the bus, my condo is way up on Twenty First Avenue," she said through a yawn, her sleepy eyes blinking heavily.

"Have you ever ridden on the back of a motorcycle?"

Cindy immediately perked up. "No, but that sounds awesome!"

She clapped her hands together, excitement wiping away the traces of exhaustion. They walked outside and he handed her his helmet. She stared at the monster of shiny black and metallic steel. He loved his bike and he could tell she was a little frightened now that she was standing in front of it.

"Are you ok?" He asked.

"Yes, let's go!"

He straddled the bike and she climbed on behind him, wrapping her arms around his waist. He started his bike and engine roared, rattling its passengers. He felt her grip grow tight when the engine rumbled and he smiled, as she pressed herself tight against him. He had to adjust to the extra weight on the bike, but found it easy and comfortable. It felt right to have her on with him, scooted up against his back and holding on tight. A new thrill raced through him.

When they pulled up to the beautiful condominium, Cade stood and stared at it in awe. The brick had been painted white, and the balcony on the second floor was wrapped in beautiful ornate cast iron. She took his hand in hers.

"Would you like to come up?" She asked as she squeezed his hand in hers.

While he very much wanted to come up, Cade knew she needed rest. He pulled her hand to his lips and then wrapped her into an embrace, kissing her deeply. She moaned into his mouth and pushed her body against his. He pulled back after a moment of losing himself to her.

"I would love to come up, but you need to sleep and if I come up, you won't get any rest this evening."

His husky voice deep with desire as he tore himself away from her. She groaned, but smiled and waved as he made himself climb on his bike. Turning away, she walked up the stone steps to her historic, but beautiful condo and disappeared through the navy front door. He waited a moment, fighting the urge to race in after her and rip her clothes off. A moment later, she stood in the balcony window and looked down at him. He started the engine and rumbled down the street.

Cindy watched Cade disappear around the corner. Her heart fluttered at the thought of him holding her. She had wanted him to come up and have his way with her. Cindy had a few lovers, but school and work had kept her busy over the years. Still, she had never had such a connection with anyone as she had Cade. He seemed to be hiding something about his past. When they had spent the night talking at the bar and after they had slept together, she had only asked a few questions about his past, but didn't seem very forthcoming with the information.

Turning away from the window, her feet and back ached, but thinking of Cade's hard muscular chest and stomach, another ache threatened to consume her. Her condo was beautiful; her own little peaceful haven. The off-white walls complimented the dark hardwood floors and the neutral tones of the tiles in the kitchen. Her kitchen was large with marbled countertops and stainless steel appliances. Her parents wanted her to live lavishly, but she never really cared for that life. She longed for something simpler.

They both had frowned at her occupation of choice. She knew they would have rather her follow her older brother's footsteps and become a doctor or surgeon. If only they knew how much work and dedication, as well sweat and tears, went into her profession. Nursing made her feel like she was contributing in a way that she didn't think she would feel if she had gone on to medical school. She had even talked of being a teacher, but mostly to make her parents squirm. Rebelling was never something she was very good at, but she did take pride in her small victories.

Now that she was alone, she could feel just how tired her body and mind were. She looked to her bedroom through the French doors, her bed was made up and waiting for her. Sara had obviously been by to clean and straighten up, which meant her fridge would be stocked. Compliments of her parents, she had her own maid and grocery shopper. She sighed and rolled her eyes. She had told Sara plenty of times not to come back and that she would survive without her, but her parents were insistent that she be taken care of.

Her mind went back to Cade. Those eyes were so penetrating and she loved his free spirit. He had a sadness in those eyes, but a strength that backed it. She was captivated by him and at the same time, she felt completely in love with him. That frightened her, since she had only just met him. His demeanor and tattoos made him seem rough and fierce. She knew if he ever met her parents they would have a conniption. But, he wanted her and she just couldn't understand why. Regardless, she loved it and she wanted more.

Opening the fridge, the cool air from inside blew out at her and she looked at the many choices of pre-cooked meals. Fresh fruits and vegetables loaded down the drawers in her fridge, and her favorite yogurts and juices lined the shelves. She took out a juice and in almost one gulp emptied the small bottle. Slowly she peeled off her scrubs and threw them in the laundry basket as she made her way to the bath to have a hot and bubbly soak. Starting her bath, she decided she wanted a glass of her pinot noir, so she wrapped herself in the softest robe and tiptoed back to her kitchen. She poured the delicious smooth red liquid into her glass and made her way back to her steamy, large claw foot tub. After nearly falling asleep more than once, she looked at her pruned fingers and decided it was time to get out of the bath.

She wrapped her hair in a tight towel and rubbed lotion all over her still moist skin. This ritual was the one thing that really seemed to ease her tension. Well, she had found another activity she would like to do more of to relax. She had been sore the next day after the best sex of her life, but she loved every inch of Cade and wanted to feel him deep in her again. She bit her lip and thought about calling him back to her condo, but decided he was being too much of a gentleman so she crawled into bed naked, as always, and fell fast asleep. Dreams of a handsome shaggy-haired man consumed her unconscious mind. A chiseled chest and a blood red dragon snaking up a muscular bicep mingled with the tangled up naked bodies in her dream. When she woke for her next shift, her mind and body were even more sexually aroused than when she had fallen asleep.

*****

That night, Cade ached with desire for Cindy. Going to bed was hard and he looked at his phone several times. Finally, he texted her.

Him: Hey what are you up to?

Her: *Hey, same as most nights, busy with the crazies!*

Him: Would you care if I came to visit sometime?

Her: No, come anytime! I can't promise I will be free, but definitely come visit. Shouldn't you be sleeping now?

Him: *I can't stop thinking about you and it makes it impossible to sleep.* He hoped that wasn't too forward.

Her: I understand, you left me pretty frustrated this afternoon.

Him: Good. Talk to you soon.

Her: Night Cade.

Him: Night Cindy.

He thought about getting up then and heading over to visit, but he didn't want to appear too desperate. They were not even a couple yet, he wasn't sure what they were, but he knew he wanted to keep her all to himself.

7

A few days later, Tommy and Heather were back in the shop.

"I love it!" Heather squealed as she looked at the fairy design.

Cade had given her a drawing of a fairy with a bright pink pixie cut who was dressed in a tattered purple dress. Her wings were blue, green, and pink and she had the perfect hour glass figure.

"Where will she be going?" Cade inquired.

Heather pointed at her thigh and Cade was surprised. The finger was a rather sensitive area and she was clearly in discomfort, he wondered how she was going to react to the soft spot on her thigh being worked on for at least an hour or more.

"This is awesome dude," Tommy complimented as he looked at the eye staring back at him.

It was black and curved and rested inside of a pyramid. Many would confuse the tattoo with a popular secret society, or maybe even the ancients, but Cade had designed it by incorporating ideas of each.

"And where will we add the eye?"

Tommy rolled up his right sleeve, exposing the nicely carved out bicep that he had worked on building up after years of drug abuse. His track marks had mostly cleared up, but some scaring still raced up his arms. Many of the tattoos that Cade had placed on his arms were to hide those very scars.

"Alright then," Cade smiled. "Let me get set up, who wants to go first?"

Tommy looked at Heather and she pointed at him. They moved back to the room and Tommy took a seat in the leather chair as Cade prepared the ink and sat the design up so he could reference it as he worked. Marking the outline points on Tommy's bicep, Cade began to craft his art. It didn't take too long, especially since he did not have a bunch of colors to add. He did have to add some shading, but after that he was done and he sat back, cleaning the area. Tommy looked at it and appraised it.

"Thanks man, it's awesome." He smiled and showed it off to Heather.

Next Heather took her seat. Cade got everything ready and marked her thigh. As he started he heard her suck in some air and Tommy came to hold her hand. It took a while, as he added the colors and the features to the fairy's face. When he was done, the area around Heather's new tattoo was slightly swollen and red with irritation from the intrusion of a foreign substance. He cleaned the area and sat back to let her examine it. Her face lit up with joy and when she got up to leave, she hugged Cade tightly.

"Thank you!" She gushed.

"You're very welcome," Cade managed to squeak out from Heather's hug.

Heather let go and pulled back before speaking again. "Cindy is coming to our house for dinner tomorrow night, would you like to join us Cade?"

"Uh, alright," Cade stammered at the unexpected question. Hearing Cindy's name, had caused Cade's heart to skip a beat. "What time?"

"Around seven."

"Do I need to bring anything?"

"Yourself and maybe a good bottle of pinot noir. That is one of her favorites."

"Ok."

Cade stored that bit of information away for safe keeping. Tommy took Heather's hand and they walked out of the shop.

Looking at the time, Cade thought Cindy might be sleeping by now. He wanted to surprise her at work tomorrow and, after debating on a good first gift, he decided to do something classic and go with flowers. He dressed himself nicely and trimmed his beard. He stopped by the grocery stores floral department and found roses and lilies in bunches. He collected a few single stem flowers that he thought went nicely together and had them wrap it with a ribbon; hoping they would survive the bike ride to the hospital.

Parking in visitors parking, he strode up to the emergency room doors. The smell of antiseptic and sanitizer invaded his senses as it had when he had to stay for a few nights. Cade grimaced at the bright white lights. He couldn't stand hospitals or clinics, they were so sterile, boring, "perfect". Walking up to administration and registration he asked for Cindy Watkins, and they pointed him down a corridor to the left.

Passing the hospital gift shop and café, he saw families enjoying meals and visitors purchasing gifts for their sick loved ones. A few nurses and doctors in scrubs sat and ate their breakfast, exhaustion clear on their faces. He continued down the corridor, passing one or two patients being pushed in a wheelchair or walking in robes with a mobile saline drip attached. He saw what looked like a nursing station and walked towards it. His heart grew excited when he saw Cindy leaning over the nurse's station, a stack of charts in front of her.

Then he stopped as a man in a white lab coat strode up to Cindy, his eyes were fixed on her bottom and he leaned against the counter on his elbow. His hair was black and slicked back and his young-looking face placed him in his late twenties, maybe early thirties. If he was in his twenties, Cade wondered how he already wore a lab coat embroidered with M.D. on the pocket. His face crinkled into a smile as he talked to Cindy. He watched as those same roving eyes moved up and down her body, not even looking at her face for more than a second. His intentions were clear. She seemed indifferent to his perverted assessment of her body. Rage bubbled in the pit of Cade's stomach and he itched to walk over and punch that smug face. He continued towards the pair.

"Hey beautiful," Cade said loudly enough to ensure the doctor also heard him clearly.

Cade smiled as Cindy turned and her face beamed when she saw him. Smug face in a lab coat frowned as he looked at Cade, his face scrunching up as if he smelled something sour. Cade presented the bouquet of flowers and the cocky doctor chuckled. Ignoring him, Cade watched Cindy's face process the gift and her smile deepened.

"They are perfect, thank you."

She reached up to kiss him on the lips and he hooked an arm around her, pulling her in close. She laughed, but squirmed as she wiggled away.

"Not at work!"

He smiled and noticed that the young doctor had disappeared.

"Don't you have like, an on-call room or something," Cade asked as he cocked a mischievous eyebrow at her.

"You have watched far too much television! Even if I said yes that we have one, it will most likely be full of sleeping interns or exhausted doctors." Just then a page came over head for her. "Looks like I gotta run. I hear you will be at the dinner tonight?"

"I will."

"See you then." She walked off with the bouquet in her hands.

***

Cindy knew what Todd was doing when she was standing at the nurse's station. She also knew that Cade was clearly jealous. It was adorable though and she thought he was rather well behaved as he made it obvious that she was his and his alone. Todd's disapproval almost cracked her up. Now he was paging her under the false pretense that there was an emergency.

"Yes Todd?" She asked, hiding her annoyance.

"It's Dr. White, and we have bedpans that need cleaning in room 318."

"Hmmm. That seems rather mundane to being paging me."

"If you were the patient, you wouldn't think so. Also, do something with the flowers before you cause a patient to go into anaphylactic shock." He shook his head.

With that, he looked at his watch and stormed off down the hall. She cursed him under breath, the arrogant fool. She used one of the pans they handed to patients to vomit in to rest her beautiful bouquet in as she went in to visit one of her patients, Mr. Hall.

"Good morning Mr. Hall, I hear you need your bedpan cleaned." She smiled as she entered the room.

Mr. Hall had been in for almost a month, a car wreck had left him widowed. He was a sweet sixty-eight-year-old man, and she enjoyed his company and his stories.

"That pompous fool could have taken it himself," his raspy voice crackled as he spoke and coughed.

Cindy tried to maintain her professional bearing, but she had to stifle her laugh as if she too was coughing.

"Well, is there anything else I can do for you Mr. Hall?"

"A large chocolate bar, you know one of those one pound blocks of sugar and cocoa in the gift shop?"

He smiled, a twinkle in his eyes, despite the tube running into his nose, feeding him.

"Oh, I would happily get that with you if you will share."

"Deal."

"Call me if you need anything dear."

With that, Cindy left, collected her flowers and made her way back to the stack of charts she had left at the nurse's station. Cade had left some time ago, and Annie looked at her from behind the counter; her dark curly hair resting against her dark skin.

"Who was that handsome fella?" She looked over her gold rimmed glasses.

Annie had been a nurse for more than thirty years. Cindy wasn't sure how she could do it for so many years, but she had and she was very knowledgeable. Any questions regarding proper nursing practices and protocols, you could find Annie and she could tell you the page and paragraph to find it.

"His name is Cade and I think we may be dating." She blushed.

"May be dating, how do you not know if you are a couple?"

"We haven't really called it anything, we have just been out two or three times, but I feel like I am falling fast for him." She leaned against the counter, slightly embarrassed about her sudden feelings for someone she only barely knew, but she felt like she had known him forever.

"Well, he sure was into you. At least he kept his eyes on your face, even if his hands were roaming." She rolled her eyes and Cindy blushed.

"He is a little rough around the edges," Cindy admitted. "But so far he seems to have a soft and kind heart."

"Just be careful young lady. Try to protect your heart, until you know his true intentions."

"Yes, ma'am."

"Don't get smart with me, I know a thing or two about what these young studs want from a pretty little lady like you." She puffed up a little as she looked at Cindy and she shook her head.

"I will be careful, you don't have to worry."

Cindy really didn't think there was anything to worry about. Cade had been the perfect gentleman so far. She checked the time and thought about what she could bring to the dinner tonight. The easiest thing would be stopping at the store and buying a pack of premade rolls, which is probably what she would do. She grabbed her phone and texted Heather.

Cindy: Hey, what do I need to bring tonight?

Heather: We could use rolls and maybe napkins. Do you think you could bring those?

Cindy: *Done! See you at seven!*
***

Cade left the hospital and went to the liquor store. Rows of wine lined the walls and in the center of the stores. He was more of a beer drinker, but he had occasionally enjoyed a glass of wine. However, he had no idea what he was looking for, other than pinot noir.

"Can I help you?" An older gentleman behind the counter stepped out with a friendly smile.

"I need to find pinot noir and I am slightly out of my element."

"Here, let's get you taken care of. Do you have a price range?"

"Um, I suppose like... thirty bucks?"

Cade didn't know, but he had heard that the higher the cost the better the quality with wine. No idea if that was true or not, but he knew that top shelf liquor was delicious.

"Let's see, here this one has a medium tannin, with notes of cherry and vanilla, it was aged in oak barrels for ten years. It is one of my best sellers."

The old man's eyes twinkled as he described the wine to Cade. Cade just smiled, wondering what a tannin was.

"Uh, Ok. I will get one bottle of that and what's your next best seller?"

"Well, I have this Sangiovese that is one of my top sellers. It's a little dry but also semi-sweet, I think you will find that your company will be most pleased."

Cade nodded and walked to the counter to pay.

"Thank you for your help sir. I am lost when it comes to wines." He gave an apologetic smile.

"No worries. I think you may find yourself surprised when you try one of these." He tucked each bottle in its own brown sack and handed them to Cade.

"Have a nice day," the shopkeeper said with a smile.

"You too."

Cade left and made his way to the shop. He had a few hours so he wanted to drop in and see how things were. Cadence stood at the front, hands on her hips in a heated conversation with a young girl.

"Honey, you have to be at least sixteen for that and then eighteen for the other. You do not have a parent or guardian here for the consent, and I am not going to risk my own job just so you can walk around with metal and holes in your body. Come back in a year when you are sixteen and we can talk."

Cade watched the young girl turn on her heel and stomp out of the shop. Teenagers could be the worst, but he remembered how hard those years were and didn't envy the youth one bit.

"Hey boss," Cadence greeted once she caught sight of Cade.

He looked at her, seeing that she had changed her hair again. She changed it so often, Cade wondered how it didn't fall out. Today she sported a short black bob cut with bright red streaks running through. She actually had minimal piercings, but a half sleeve covered her bicep and she had been talking about covering her other arm sometime soon.

"Hey, scaring off potentials I see." He laughed at her, giving her a hard time. "Is Alex in the back?"

"Yup."

He walked to the back room and found Alex deep in work on a customer's forearm.

"That looks good," Cade complimented as he looked at the design taking life on the man's forearm. Alex just grunted and continued.

When Cade returned to the front of the store, he thought he caught a glimpse of a shiny shaved head with a strip of hair down the center. He ran outside, but saw nobody on the sidewalk. He ran his fingers through his hair and touched his beard. If that kid really was looking for him from the fight, he wanted to know what the hell the kid wanted. If it was another fight, Cade would be happy to kick his ass again, but he didn't need some kid stalking him.

His phone vibrated and a message from Cindy lit up the screen. It was a picture attachment, he opened it. Her flowers sat in a vase on top of a nice marbled counter top. He assumed inside of her apartment. He put his phone back in his pocket and gathered his things. He wasn't afraid of the kid, but he wanted to know what was going on. He had fought many sore losers in the past, but none resorted to stalking him. It was creepy more than anything.

Cade headed home to get ready for the dinner at Heather and Tommy's. There wasn't a special occasion that he could think of, but he was excited that he would get to see Cindy again. Back at his apartment, he had to pick out a nice outfit. He didn't want anything too casual or too formal, but he wanted to look good. The time ticked down until he had to hop on his bike and head over. Once there, he parked his bike on the curb and walked up towards the two story brick home they had purchased a couple years ago. There was a sign by the front door now that read Mr. and Mrs. Tommy Lane, est. April 2016. He smiled at their sign and knocked on the door.

Heather opened her door and Cade stepped into the foyer of their home. There was a chandler over the large stairwell and their dog Rosco came running around the corner of the stairs to sniff the intruder. He took off his leather coat and hung it up on the coat rack by the door. Following Heather into the kitchen, he placed both bottles of wine on the counter. The smell of food was intoxicating his senses as he moved to the dining room table. Cindy was running late. Almost thirty minutes later she knocked on the door and stormed in, apologizing. They had waited on her and were more than ready to dig in when she came through the door.

Sitting around the table, conversation erupted. Cade watched Cindy and smiled. She had worn a little red dress and had tied her hair back again. His mind raced with ideas of what was under that pretty little red dress.

"Cade, hey, Cade." Tommy was calling his name and Cade nearly had to shake himself from his daydream. "We have a cruise planned for this fourth of July, do you think you could keep Rosco for us?"

Cade looked at the drooling brown mutt in the corner. He had kept the dog before, and was fine with doing so again. Rosco's tail began wagging at the mention of his name.

"Of course. Where are you guys going?" They looked at each other and smiled.

"Alaska!" The word came in unison.

"Well that sounds fun!"

Their conversations continued and unfortunately, family became the topic.

"Well, my big brother is doing just fine as the doctor in the family. I am happy as the nurse," Cindy finished.

Cade had listened to Cindy talk about her wealthy family. Her parents sounded disappointed in her career choice, but he couldn't understand why.

"What about you Cade, any siblings?" She took another bite of food.

"No, just me," he kept short.

"Were your parents supportive of you and your art?"

She was prying again. She had pried before and he had not given any information, but he would eventually have to share his background he assumed.

"My parents died when I was four, I don't talk about it too much." He shrugged and took a sip of the Pinot Noir, it was delicious as the salesman had said.

"Oh, I am sorry, was it an accident?"

Her eyes were full of pain and sorrow. He didn't want her or anyone to feel sorry for him, and he felt guilty that he was growing angry at her questioning.

"Uh, yea, an accident."

He put down his fork and took a big sip of his wine. He hoped she would get the idea, and was thankful that she did. Her eyes still seemed pained, but she didn't press any further.

"Hey, we have cake!" Tommy interrupted and jumped up and ran to the kitchen.

They sat in silence and waited. Cade hoped that Cindy would not look at him differently now, like so many had before.

After the dinner, they both stood on the front porch and told their two friends good night. They looked at each other and he placed an arm around her waist. She leaned against him and he felt her rest her weight against him.

"I am sorry," she whispered. "I didn't mean…. I didn't know."

"It's ok," Cade assured as he stroked her hair. "I will tell you about my family, just not tonight, ok?"

He rested his bearded cheek against her head and felt her nod. They made their way down the steps to his bike. He wrapped his jacket around her and placed his helmet on her head. They rumbled down the street towards her condo. At the curb, she held his hand and looked at him, the sadness was no longer in her eyes. A heat had filled those bright blues and he felt that same desire began to throb as he looked at her in that tight little red dress.

"Would you like to come up tonight?" Her husky voice practically purred.

"Yes," was his instant reply.

He followed her up the stone steps and through the large navy door. Inside, the condo was huge and very well polished. Her décor was clean and crisp and he was slightly overwhelmed by the prosperity of it all. While he had been distracted soaking in his surroundings, he had not even noticed she was standing on the steps waiting for him to join her. He followed her up to the second floor, where a large king bed invited him to curl up in its soft sheets.

"Would you like anything to drink?" Her bright eyes seemed nervous, as if this was not their second time but their first.

"Maybe later."

He walked towards her and pulled her in close, kissing her and stealing the breath right from her. She tasted warm and sweet tonight, hints of wine on her tongue. She stepped back and turned so he could slowly unzip her little red dress, allowing it to fall to the ground. Her black strapless bra and red underwear enticing him as he unclasped the back of her bra and allowed her breasts to fall free from their confinement. He reached around and caressed the soft skin, lightly pinching her hard and inviting nipple. She sucked in a breath as he moved down to pull her red underwear down. She turned and surprised him as she pressed against him, kissing him and pulling his shirt up in a fevered attempt to undress him faster.

Her hands fussed with the button of his jeans and he helped her unsteady hands as he stripped the rest of the way down. Then he pulled her in close, feeling the warmth of her naked skin against his own and relishing their closeness. His hard cock throbbing against her thigh, he was trying hard not to bend her over and pound her from behind. He wanted to take his time, but he was also aching to be inside her.

Before he even knew what she was doing, she bent down on her knees and took him in her mouth. Her tongue licking his large head as she wrapped her hands around his shaft. She squeezed and sucked at the same time. He thought he was going to lose his mind from the ripples of pleasure that shot up and down his body and he felt his legs grow weak. He reached down and pulled her up to stand against him again and he kissed her as he guided her down on her large bed. She had teased him, it was his turn. He kissed her neck and moved down the length of her body only stopping to flick his tongue against her hard nipples and then finding her perfect pink center, glistening with desire.

He spread her legs and kissed her as he plunged his tongue inside, licking and tasting her. She tasted so good and her moans drove him wild. Finally, feeling her tightening, he moved back up to her and kissed her as he thrust between her legs. She cried out as his large raw cock filled her completely. He felt her naturally ribbed and soft center wrap tight around him and with each buck of his hips, she tightened until she screamed out and waves of pulsating pleasure radiated from deep within.

"How do you want me?" Her husky voice whispered and panted in his ear as she nibbled softly. He groaned and could barely think straight, her orgasm nearly sending him over the edge.

"Bend over."

He rolled away as she got into position, her perfect round bottom and wide hips inviting him to come inside. She was on all fours but he got a good glimpse of her breast as they rested against the bed and her dreamy, pleasure filled eyes watched him. He got behind her and ran his hands over her smooth hips, she moaned. He felt between her legs, ensuring she was wet and ready for him as he thrust deep from behind. Every penetration she cried out and squeezed the sheets. She was so tight that around him. He reached around and played with her nipples, as he thrust his large throbbing member as far into her as possible. Her body shook and he felt another wave of tightening and pulsating as she went completely liquid on him.

He sat back, his legs burning from the work and she climbed on top of him straddling him and grinding her hips down on him. He moaned as she sent him over the edge, filling her with his own hot orgasm, he throbbed inside of her as she collapsed on him, never wanting to leave that warm pulsing wet center. They were both out of breath as they lying back on the pillows. She rolled over to rest her head on his chest and he wrapped his arm around her.

"That was wonderful," she moaned and kissed his chest.

"Mmm," was his response.

"Cade?"

"Hmm?" He answered, again without words.

"I want more."

He turned his head to her and smiled. His eyes flush with lust.

"I will give you more tonight, don't worry."

She grinned and rolled on top of him, meaning she wanted more right then. He was surprised that within a few minutes he was just as hard as the first time and ready to go. They made love again, but this time they both passed out after, a tangled mess of sweaty bodies and sheets.

8

Cade and Cindy were awoken from their slumber by a horrified gasp. Cindy sat up terrified, and pulled the sheets nearly above her head. Cade had also bolted upright and covered himself with a pillow. Cindy's mother stood in her daughter's bedroom and gawked at her. Without a word, her pale mother left the room and rushed down the stairs. Cindy groaned and Cade sat there with his mouth wide open in shock.

"Was that?" He started.

"Yes, my mother," she groaned again and climbed out of bed.

"You would think I was some teenager the way they coddled me, not a grown woman," she sighed and began dressing herself.

"I suppose meeting your family is going to go over far worse than I had already assumed," Cade chuckled.

"Quite possibly. Now that she has seen my boyfriend naked, I guess I should formally introduce you to her... them." She smiled mischievously at him, but pulled up short as she realized she had just called him her boyfriend. "Oh, I am sorry. I can't believe I just said that."

She blushed and turned to go make morning coffee.

"Don't be, I like the sound of it," he purred to her as he walked up behind her and kissed her on the cheek.

"I will see if we can have dinner with them soon, so you can meet them."

She smiled. He half smiled back. They had breakfast, which Cade left after. She ignored her mother's texts and calls all day; letting the woman stew for a while. Cindy wanted to teach her that she shouldn't come barging into her grown daughter's condo. Though Cindy knew she would eventually have to acknowledge her and she wanted them to meet Cade. She was falling pretty fast for him and she would want their approval. She was worried they would have a hard time with his profession and his tattoos, but if they could get to know him, she was sure they would love him like she did.

Cade wasn't sure how to repair the damage from that morning with Cindy's mom. Their first meeting had gone over so splendid. He shook his head. He didn't know if that was how normal parent's behaved or not. He felt like they may be a little overbearing, but then again, he had never experienced overbearing parents. He needed to clear his head though, so he made his way to the shop and quickly distracted himself with his art. A few requests were sent in and he started their designs, sketching out the first few.

He read the text from Cindy and felt his heart hit his stomach. She had apparently made plans for a family dinner and introduction to her new boyfriend this weekend. This would be interesting. When he woke up from the sudden horrified gasp that morning, he was shocked to see an older blonde with the same bright blue eyes as Cindy staring at him. They could have passed as sisters. Now he was invited to meet the same woman, face to face, and he was scared as hell at what she would think of him. Then again, why should he be scared? She was a grown woman, surely her mother knew she wasn't an innocent virginal woman, holding out till her wedding night.

His mind was so distracted he hadn't heard the bell over the door ring, until a thin, pale-skinned girl stood at the front counter. Her hair was bright green and her face held multiple piercings, from the snake bites under her lip, to her septum, to a row of rings lining her eyebrows. Those blue eyes stared at Cade, unblinking. He was felt a chill at those empty brown dots.

"Can I help you?" Cade inquired.

"Are you Cade?" Her voice was empty of any emotion.

"Who's asking?"

"Spencer has been going crazy after you kicked his ass dude."

"Spencer?"

"At the night club. Anyways, I was supposed to deliver you a message."

She pulled out a crumpled piece of paper and handed it over to him. Her tiny hands were filthy and her nails had clumps of maybe dirt or other foreign matter under them. She was about as grunge as she could be. Cade uncrumpled the paper and looked at the random symbols, not able to make any sense of them.

"Hey what does this…mean?" Cade began to ask, but a ring from the bell over the door signaled that she had left.

Alone with the obscure message, he balled it up and tossed it in the garbage. This was all so bizarre. After he had dinner with Cindy and her parents this weekend, he would have to head down to the club and hope this "Spencer" would be there.

"We are heading out, don't stay too late boss," Cadence called as she and Alex arrived at the lobby of the shop.

She reached over tousling his shaggy brown hair and then took Alex by the arm as they left the shop. He saw her steal a quick kiss from Alex once outside and wondered when the two had started dating. They were a perfect fit and he wondered what had taken them so long in the first place. He looked at his phone and messaged

Cindy that he would come with her to her parents this weekend.

Looking at the clock, he hadn't realized how late it was, so he shut off all of the lights and locked the doors for the night. He considered taking a ride through town, but was more exhausted than he realized.

Probably the long night of love making with Cindy. He concluded.

She had drained him last night and he smiled at the thought of it. Climbing onto his bike, his heart raced and he brought the loud engine to life and sped down the road, and away from the city.

Lou Lou's lights were blinking as usual and the lineup of bikes was familiar and inviting. Cade parked his bike in the usual spot and walked into the bar. At the bar, he saw the same little bartender that he had rescued a couple months back, serving drinks. Her clothes were more modest than before and he didn't see her flirting with the customers. He took a seat at the bar and waited for her to take his order. Recognition sparked in her eyes when she came to him and she smiled at him.

"Hey, you haven't been in here for a little minute." She smiled and poured him a cold draft of pale ale, he was surprised she remembered.

"I have been busy."

He hadn't been in a relationship in a long time, but the way the little bartender still looked at him made him feel guilty for even coming to Lou Lou's. Just then, a hand tapped him on the shoulder and he turned to find Jimmy.

"Hey man, I just wanted to say thank you." Jimmy tucked his hands in his pockets and looked at his toes. "Also, that I am sorry."

"It's ok Jimmy, but did you ever apologize to the lady?" He turned his head toward the bartender.

"Oh, yes I did. I felt real bad for the way I acted."

"Just mind how much you drink," Cade chided.

"Oh, I do now."

"Good to hear. See you around Jimmy, take care now."

He turned back to his beer and the little bartender had moved on down the line. He finished his beer and decided that Lou Lou's wasn't where he wanted to spend his time. Cindy was where he wanted to be and he felt wrong having another woman eye him the way the little lady serving drinks had. Stepping outside he realized he hadn't smoked in weeks, at least not since before the fight.

Have I been so distracted that I haven't needed a cigarette?

Inside the pouch on his bike, he pulled out a pack of smokes and pulled one smoke out, fingering it in his hand. No craving or desire filled him like it had once. Crumpling the pack, he walked to the trashcan outside the club and threw the box away. He had considered breaking the habit on many occasions, but had never found the motivation. Cindy made him want to be better. He climbed on his bike and left behind Lou Lou's. Sad that he was not satisfied with his old hangout, but excited to see where things would go with Cindy. He rode back into the city and made his way to his apartment.

***

That weekend he met Cindy at her condo and they rode to her parents. Once again he found himself in wine country, not far from the winery that Tommy and Heather were married. When he turned on the driveway to her parent's estate, they had to punch in a code at the large wrought iron gates that held a huge gold embossed 'W' in the center. His bike rattled across the cobble stone drive way and he stared at the huge mansion before him. He wondered just how much money these people had. Their land stretched for miles in each direction and he saw stables in the distance and hurdles set up for jumping show horses.

They stopped in front of the miniature castle, at least that is what he equated it to, and he parked his bike. Suddenly, Cade felt very under dressed to even set foot in such an estate. Her parents stepped out on the large porch and welcomed them between the giant marble columns that lined the front of the house. Cade shook her father's hand and her mother's. Her mother's lips were pinched tight in disapproval, but she shook his hand nonetheless. Her father's face also shone with disapproval, and something else. Cindy hugged her mother and kissed her father on the cheek.

Her and her mother looked almost identical, but her father looked nothing like her. His salt and pepper hair was kept short and neat and his face was clean shaven. His stony face was sharp and angular and he clearly took care of his physical health as well as his financial. Mr. Watkins had an arrogant and over confident air to him, much like that youthful doctor at the hospital.

They moved inside the mansion and just as he had felt overwhelmed by the elegance of Cindy's condo, the interior of her family home was even more extravagant. A wide mouthed stairwell greeted them when they entered and ran up to the second floor, narrowing in the middle and widening again at the top just as it did at the bottom. A huge shimmery chandelier hung above them as they walked across the marbled floors. Cindy and her other moved down one hallway and she signaled for him to follow her father. They moved into the study and Cindy's father took out two glasses and poured some dark, expensive looking liquid in them. Handing one to Cade, he raised the glass to his upper lip and breathed in the strong scent of the liquor. Swirling it in the glass he brought it to his mouth and sipped.

Cade looked down at the glass and copied Mr. Watkins. It burned as it hit his throat and his taste buds picked up the smoke and cherry notes of the strong drink. A large fireplace with an ornate mantle sat in the center of the room. Cade held the glass in his hands and wondered when someone would break the silence.

"So, I hear you and my daughter are dating." Mr. Watkins voice was higher in pitch than Cade had expected.

"I, yes. We met at our mutual friend's wedding a few weeks back. I have enjoyed her company." He took another small sip of the harsh liquid, burning his throat again.

"I bet." Her father's face showed no hint of humor.

"Your estate is lovely. What is it that you do, sir?" He wasn't sure how to ask such a question, but the man was evidently wealthy. He was genuinely curious as to how he made his fortune.

"What I 'do', is many things. I own several large companies and a few franchises. That mixed with my savvy investing, I have been able to build quite the fortune for my children and hopefully one day my grandchildren."

Cade almost choked as he processed the last part. Grandchildren? He hadn't even thought about having children. Well, he had, but never any serious thoughts.

"And what is it, that you do, Mr...?"

Cade realized they had not been introduced. Everything was going so horribly wrong he thought.

"Mr. Cade Winters, and I run a fairly prestigious tattoo parlor in the heart of the city."

He felt very proud of his own business venture, no matter how small it was compared to this tycoon before him.

"Hmm," Her father grunted and raised his eyebrows in mock amusement; clearly not impressed with Cade.

They stood in silence and Cade wondered where Cindy and her mother had disappeared to. Just then, Cindy stormed into the study, her eyes were alight with anger.

"Supper is ready," She growled and stalked over to Cade; wrapping her arm in his.

They ate in silence, the awkward clink of silverware as it brushed against the fine china nearly echoed from the absence of noise.

"So, Cindy, have you thought anymore about finishing up that medical degree?" Her father wiped his mouth and sat back from his plate, taking a long drink from his glass of water.

"Well, as I have told you before," Cindy sighed while rolling her eyes. "I love being a nurse and I love what I do. So, no."

"You graduated the top of your class in pre-med!" Her mother interjected and placed another piece of the juicy speared meat in her mouth, slowly chewing and placing her fork back down on her napkin between each bite.

"She saved a life a few weeks ago. A stab victim came in and she worked quickly to save his life," Cade defended.

He smiled at her, anger with her parents bubbling beneath the surface. She squeezed his thigh under the table. Cade wasn't sure if she was thanking him or shushing him. He waited for any response from her parents, but they acted as if he had said nothing at all.

"Well, you really should consider going back before you get too old," Her father continued with his line of thought. "The longer you are out of school the more information you will lose."

Her parents didn't even look at him as they continued to try and plan her future.

"How is Todd?" Her mother asked as she looked at Cade, a darkness flashed behind her eyes and then she looked at Cindy conspiratorially.

"Mother, you know that ended ages ago."

Cindy's cheeks burned and Cade wondered who Todd was.

"He was so handsome and a successful doctor at your work. I know you still work with him. I spoke with him the other day and asked about you, since you ignore my calls. He said some shaggy haired man covered in tattoos brought you flowers and that was what prompted me to visit you the other morning."

Cindy's mother narrowed her eyes at Cade and it was his turn to turn bright red. He now realized that Todd was the smug doctor ogling Cindy. It bothered him that they had apparently been a couple, but that was her past so he put it behind him.

"Did he mention the bedpans?" Cindy muttered under breath.

"What? Don't mumble dear, it is truly un-lady like."

Her mother took a sip of her wine and sat back, a satisfied look on her face. Cade was more upset now by her parent's treatment of Cindy than he was of being found naked in her bed by her mother.

"What is wrong with you?" Cade lashed out, anger taking over his ability to bite his tongue.

"Excuse me?" Aghast, her mother dropped her jaw and held her hand to her chest in a dramatic gesture of shock by the anger in his voice.

"I said, what is wrong with you? Your daughter works hard to save lives day in and day out. She breaks her back to provide care to those in need. Their first moments spent in an emergency room and their last moments on earth are spent in the presence of your beautiful, smart, and talented daughter. If anything, you should be through the roof with pride over her sacrifices and accomplishments."

Cade instantly regretted losing his temper, but he couldn't understand how they could treat her this way.

"You may not be able to understand what I am about to say," Cindy's father chastised, cocking his head slightly to the side. "I assume you have a rather limited vocabulary, seeing how 'running a fairly prestigious tattoo shop' doesn't even require a two-year degree, but we aspire for excellence in this house. Now, while we are proud of Cindy's accomplishments, we expect her to shoot higher than the bottom of the rung. Of course, seeing her current love interest, we think maybe we missed an important part of her development that we managed to work into her older brother." Her father stood up and buttoned his coat. "Now, I believe you should remove yourself from our home. I have found your company to be distasteful and beneath my daughter."

Her mother also left the table and Cindy sat there, anger brewing behind those bright blues. Cade stood and reached a hand down to Cindy, but she did not take it. Without a word, she stood up and walked out the door. Cade followed behind as they made their way out the front and to his bike.

"Cindy," he started.

"Don't," She stopped him. "Just, take me home please."

Obviously, she was angry at everyone. So he climbed on his bike and she climbed on behind him. Her grip was not as tight as it had been before. When he pulled up to her condo, she hopped off and stormed towards the door. He looked after her, not sure if he should chase her or leave her be. Deciding it was best to let her stew on her own, he sped off towards his own apartment.

9

Days passed without a text message or call. Cade couldn't understand why she was mad at him. Her parents were verbally attacking her. He couldn't just sit and let them do that. He always protected the ones he cared for. It was just his nature. He regretted tossing those smokes at Lou Lou's and ripped his apartment upside down looking for a pack. There wasn't a single piece of paper wrapped around tobacco in his apartment, so he went down to the corner store and bought a pack. It had been weeks since he felt the cool burn hit his throat and he inhaled deep to enjoy the full effects of the nicotine.

Angry, and a little hurt, he made his way towards the club. A fight would help him relieve some tension. Tank was surprised to see him.

"Hey, you look miserable." Tank patted Cade on the shoulder.

"Thanks?"

"Woman troubles?"

"How could you?"

"Trust me, every man that looks and smells like you do, just had a fight with the old ball and chain."

"It was pretty bad. I am not sure how to fix it," he sighed.

"You will figure it out, or you will find a new ball to chain yourself to," he laughed at his own joke, but Cade just smiled to be polite.

His heart wasn't in it tonight. It also wasn't in the fight. For the first time, his record was almost blemished. He only won because the young man was so exhausted, he let his guard down for just a moment and Cade attacked. Exhausted, Cade collected his earnings and sat at the bar with Tank, drinking beer after beer until his head hurt.

Stumbling out from the bar, Cade looked at his bike. He knew he shouldn't even attempt it, so he started for his apartment on foot. Once inside, he crashed fully clothed on his couch, asleep before his body was fully horizontal.

Cade awoke the next morning to a splitting migraine and a puddle of his own drool. His phone flashed that he had several new messages. Tommy had tried to contact him at strange hours and Cade listened to the first voicemail.

"You have two new voicemails, first message."

"Hey man, call me when you get this, it's urgent."

"Message deleted. Next message."

"Hey Cade, you really need to call us, something is wrong with Cindy."

"To replay your message hit '4'"

"Hey Cade, you really need to call us, something is wrong with Cindy."

Cade's heart was racing as he played the same message over and over. He hung up and called Tommy.

"Hey man, are you ok?" Tommy's worried voice boomed over the receiver.

Cade pulled his phone back from his ear a bit, trying to keep Tommy's voice from making his head feel worse.

"Yea," Cade finally responded. "What's going on, what's wrong with Cindy?"

"We don't know," Tommy said quickly. "Her parents tried calling us after they hadn't heard from her and we went to her condo and work, nobody has seen her. We have called the police, but they said it had to be over so many hours before we could actually report her as missing."

Cade's hands shook as he felt his stomach toss and turn. His nerves mixed with last night's drinking binge made him feel nauseous.

"Cade, are you there?"

"Yeah, I am. Listen, I have to go."

He hung up and ran to the sink to splash water on his face. He had never felt as scared in his life as he did right now.

Where is she… is she ok?

He needed to run by her place to make sure nothing had been missed. As fast as he could, Cade ran down the few blocks to Tank's nightclub and he jumped on his bike. Revving the engine, he sped to her place. Tommy, Heather, her parents, and a police cruiser sat outside her elegant condo. He rushed up to them and her parents looked at him accusingly.

"Did you do something to our daughter?" Her father grabbed Cade by the collar, but he shoved the man's hands away.

"I would never do anything to hurt Cindy. I love her!"

Shocked to say the words out loud, Cade was interrupted from his thoughts by a cop walking back from the condo with a crumpled piece of paper in her hands.

"What's that?" Cade asked, pointing at the paper.

"We can't figure it out. There's a bunch of squiggly shapes and symbols, but nothing makes sense." The officer shook her head and headed for her partner to show him the paper.

Cade's heart hit his stomach for real this time and he lost whatever contents remained all over the lawn and sidewalk.

"I know who has taken her," he whispered, his mind swimming with thoughts of what that crazed and murderous fool might do to her.

"What did you say Cade?" Heather leaned in towards him.

"I know who has taken Cindy," he said louder.

"Who?" Her father crossed his arms and waited, trying not to strangle the information out of Cade.

"I fought a kid several weeks back at an underground nightclub. All I know is his name is Spencer and he is apparently obsessed with me. The stab victim I told you Cindy saved, was me. I was stabbed in the alley behind the nightclub, and I am certain it was that kid that I fought who stabbed me. Cindy was the first person I saw in my delirium, but I didn't see her again until Tommy and Heather's wedding. Spencer sent a scrawny young lady to my shop last week and had her deliver me a message. It was exactly like this one; a chaos of scribbles and symbols with no rhyme or reason."

His stomach was still queasy and Cade knelt to try and stead himself. One of the two cops had overheard him retell the whole story and approached Cade.

"Could you describe this 'Spencer'?"

"Yes," he declared. "I know exactly what he looks like."

"Well come with us to the station. We need a full report, including where you were last night and someone to back your alibi. Also, we need to get you in front of the facial recognition artist, and have him cross your description across the database for any known records or violations."

Cade nodded and followed the cop's instructions. He would do anything if it meant getting Cindy back safe.

After supplying the cops with his alibi, backed by Tank, Cade also made sure the artists were given the clearest and most detailed description of 'Spencer'. They quickly found a record matching Cade's description. When they pulled up his file, Cade knew it was the same young man from before. He nodded when asked if this was the one who had left him to die.

"That's the little sick bastard, yes."

Cade touched his now mostly healed side. Where it once burned, and ached, it was now just a tender memory of the pain.

"Spencer Flemming, age twenty-six," the Cop recited. "He has been busted on several accounts of assault and possession. He has been in and out of treatment facilities for a mental condition. Not sure what."

With each word read, Cade grew more concerned for Cindy's safety. When they were finally done questioning Cade, he left the precinct and made his way towards Tank's. It was too early for the club to be open, but Cade knew that Tank lived above the club. Cade texted him and waited in the alley he was once stabbed in, the rancid smell of the dumpster just as bad as that night. A series of locks moved and rotated, let Cade know that Tank was just on the other side.

"What do you want Cade?" His voice was gruff and lacked the usual friendliness to it.

"Tank, do you keep any information on the fighters? I remembered we left our addresses on a sheet once and our phone numbers. I am looking for someone, I think he has Cindy."

Cade didn't know if he was making any sense and by the look on Tank's face, he was sure he wasn't.

"Cindy?" Tank questioned.

"Yes, Cindy. Look, I believe Spencer has her and I have to find her before he hurts her."

Tank must have seen the pleading behind Cade's eyes, because he sighed and ushered him inside.

"You know, cops have been sniffing around here. Did you and this Cindy have anything to do with it?"

Cade winced and nodded.

"I am sorry Tank, but I must find Cindy. I gave them information about Spencer and our fight. I wasn't even thinking about what that could potentially do to your business."

Cade was truly sorry, but he his mind raced with saving his girl.

"Look, I am going to help you, because you are a really nice guy. I have always liked you. But after this, you are no longer welcome here. I do not need to have the cops sniffing around and scaring off my customers. What did you say the name of this kid is?"

"Spencer, Spencer Flemming," Cade choked out.

Tank rifled through some papers and a beaten-up ledger. Names, addresses, and phone numbers of his recurring fighters were listed in surprisingly neat handwriting. Cade wondered why he had this tracking method, but he figured it might have something to do with tracking down anyone that didn't pay their dues. Tank ran his large finger down the list and after a few moments and a few page turns, he found Spencer's information. The police station had a different mailing address, which wasn't surprising to Cade. This kid was trouble and he would obviously have no issues lying to the law. Tank handed him a piece of paper with the address copied over and he rested his hand on his shoulder.

"I hope you find your girl and not a single hair on her head has been harmed. Take care of yourself Cade. You are one of the scrappiest damn fighters I have ever seen and you will be missed in the ring."

Cade smiled at Tank and thanked him one more time. With that, he left and hopped on his bike. He needed a weapon, preferably nothing sharp or loaded. He didn't need to add homicide to his record. Just then a message from Cindy flashed on his phone. Excitement bubbled up, but was quickly replaced with true terror as he opened the attachment. A picture of Cindy with a gag in her mouth, tears streaming down her face filled his screen and was forever burned into his memory. Anger fueled him as he stopped by a store and bought a thick wooden baseball bat.

His phone guided him to the address that Tank had provided. He parked his bike and walked towards the old abandoned warehouse. Windows were broken on many floors and some were boarded up. Broken bottles littered the ground and a few bodies slept under layers of clothing and ratty blankets around the outside of the building. He entered through one broken doorway and was met with a gutted interior. He checked the picture of Cindy again and recognized the same run down building he was now standing in, falling apart in the background of her scared profile.

Cade walked around, not finding anyone on the first floor and then moving towards the next. Debris littered the floors, and exposed insulation hung freely from the ceiling and walls. Some had been ripped in areas and he could see them piled up in corners, like fluffy beds. The same symbols and scribbling from the crumpled papers were scattered across the surfaces. The second floor was all open and Cade did not see Cindy anywhere, so he made his way up the creaky falling rotting away stairs to the third floor.

Every corner was stuffed with trash and more of those symbols. He felt a chill as he looked down the long corridor of doors. All, but one stood wide open. He heard a soft sob from the closed door and inched his way towards it, bat ready to swing at any assailants. He lightly pushed open the door and found Cindy tied to a chair. He rushed to her, not even caring or considering this may be a trap. She sobbed and shook all over as he removed the gag from her mouth.

"Are you ok?" He asked her with pained eyes.

She only nodded and sobbed a little more. He kissed her on the top of the head and began working to untie the knots that wrapped around her arms and the back of the chair. Releasing her from her bonds. They hurriedly ran through the door, but were stopped by a thin, scrawny grunge girl.

"Where is Spencer?" Cade demanded.

"Spencer? Spencer who?" She laughed maniacally and Cade spotted her two tiny pupils, constricted from some sort of drug.

They easily pushed passed her still cackling form and made their way down the steps. As they were descending the stairs, they stopped and looked at the scrawny, shadowed figure standing in the middle of the first floor. Spencer stepped out from the shadows and stretched his arms behind his head.

"Hello Cade. I am happy you followed the crumbs." He smiled.

Cade shook his head, this kid was more sick than he had realized. He needed to get Cindy out of here, but he also needed to kick this kid's ass and make sure he was checked into a mental facility.

Spencer swept his arms around the room, directing their eyes to the walls where his scribbles and spray paint covered every inch possible. Cade wondered how long this kid had been here, driving himself mad, and why fighting Cade had triggered the mania in him to the point of assault and kidnapping.

"You are sick Spencer," Cade called out and tucked Cindy behind him protectively.

"My name is not Spencer!"

His small frame shook and he grabbed the sides of his head, his knuckles white, spittle forming on the corner of his mouth as he screamed in rage. Cade continued to inch towards him, not wanting to upset him any further, he put his hands up in an attempt to calm the kid.

"What is your name then?" Cade asked, trying to reason with 'Spencer'.

Cindy stayed close behind him, until he put his hand on her, stopping her forward movement. He lightly touched her arm, hoping she would not follow any closer.

"It doesn't matter, names, words, letters, numbers, it doesn't matter! It's all connected into one infinite eternity of space, time, and matter. Funny, that it doesn't matter, but it is just that, matter." He began laughing hysterically and Cade gave up following his ramblings.

"Look, I do not want to hurt you, but I will if I have to."

Cade didn't feel good about attacking the kid, now that he had a chance to witness his insanity, but he would do anything to get Cindy out of there. By now, Cade was standing a few feet away from Spencer. His pupils clearly dilated and his face was twisted in a wicked grin.

"You can't hurt me Cade. Pain is fleeting. Have you ever been strapped to a chair, leather manacles holding you in place as a fat nurse pushed an eighteen-gauge needle full of thick liquid into your veins, not sure if it was day or night? What about clawing at the walls of your cell, hoping the voices in your head would stop screaming that everyone was out to get you? I have, the voices are the worst. Whispers that come and go, dark and twisting. Then, exploding into screams and fits of terror. I never know when the voices will erupt. They told me to kill you. I tried to… but you didn't die!"

Spencer lunged at Cade, but Cade quickly stepped to the side and Spencer crashed into a trash can, the rattle echoing throughout the building. Cindy squealed at the loud sound, and the skinny grungy girl from earler was watching from above, laughing maniacally. Cade wondered what they could possibly be on, to be this delirious. Spencer growled as he came back to his feet and charged Cade again. This time, Cade waited until Spencer was on him and he swung the bat, hitting him in the ribs. Spencer went down, and Cade brought a knee to his head. He didn't want to severely hurt the kid, but he wanted Spencer to be incapacitated for a moment. To his surprise, the kid hit the floor and laughed as he coughed and held his side in pain. Normally that would have surely knocked someone out, but Cade assumed the drugs had something to do with it.

"Stay down, Spencer," Cade demanded.

Wobbling to his feet, Spencer stood up and pointed his fingers in a gun motion towards Cade, pretending to pull an imaginary trigger. Cade approached Spencer and punched him in his nose, an audible crunch could be heard and the kid fell back on the floor. His eyes rolled back and he was finally out. The grunge girl was in a fit on the floor upstairs, the hilarity of scene sending her in uncontrollable stitches. Cade signaled for Cindy to follow him and they rushed out of the warehouse. She was sobbing still, clearly traumatized by the whole thing.

Cade called 911 and explained the situation to an operator. Not even five minutes later, sirens sounded and he saw the ambulance and cop cars speed around the corner. When the emergency personnel jumped down from the ambulance, they pulled a stretcher and rushed into the building where Cade had directed them to the still passed out form of Spencer.

"He is clearly messed up on some kind of drugs, and evidently mentally unstable," Cade stated to the EMTs.

"Is she ok?" They pointed up the stairs at the new sleeping form of the grunge girl.

"Honestly, I have no idea," Cade said, shaking his head. "She was laughing hysterically the entire time."

"Ok, and the girl that is with you?"

"She should also be seen I think," Cade said, glancing towards Cindy. "She was just kidnapped and I haven't had a chance to ask if he did anything to her."

A sickness formed in the pit of his stomach, twisting and turning until he felt like he would vomit. If Spencer had touched her inappropriately, he would find the little bastard and kill him. It was bad enough to know she had been scared to death from the whole ordeal, tied to a chair so tight she had rope burns on her wrists, and gagged. He couldn't allow himself to imagine anything else.

"You are going to have to come with us," a young deputy said as he stepped forward.

They questioned Cade again off to the side of the EMTs who were just pulling Spencer's unconscious body from the warehouse. He explained what he knew and had seen. They took down his information and Cade made his way back to Cindy's side. She stood beside the ambulance, as they loaded Spencer in to the back of the ambulance. They had also decided to take in the scrawny grunge girl, and Cade heard "overdose" a few times. Those words brought Cade back to his parent's death. Not allowing himself to think about such things at the moment, he turned to Cindy.

"Cindy, do you want me to call your parents?" He reached for her shaking hands, but she pulled back. He let his own hands fall to his sides feeling useless. "Cindy, I can call them for you," he reiterated.

She nodded slowly, and he took her phone, looking for her parent's number. Her parents were upset but relieved that she had been found. They demanded to know where she was, and he explained, but warned that they may be taking her to the hospital for evaluation.

Cade followed behind the emergency vehicles. He wasn't going to leave her side if he could help it.

Since he wasn't family, the hospital staff wouldn't let him back with Cindy. When her parents came in they ran straight to administration, ignoring him and were quickly taken back. He waited in the lobby for what felt like hours. When they did come back through, Cindy wore her father's coat and he stood to go to her. Cindy's mother gave a curt shake of her head, making Cade stop and watch as they walked out together. Cindy's crystal blue eyes locked with his and his heart skipped a beat. Pain threatening to overtake him as he wanted to wrap his arms around her and hold her tight.

10

As the days passed by, Cade grew restless. His beard was unruly and his staff were frustrated.

"Have you seen this week's schedule?" Cadence slammed the calendar on the counter, shaking Cade from his thoughts.

Cade glanced at the booked week. "Oh," was his only reply.

"Oh? Oh? You need to hire two more artists Cade. We cannot keep up this momentum. Our work will start getting sloppy at this rate."

Cadence placed her hands on her hips, her bright green hair drawing his attention from the full schedule.

"Your hair looks great," he deflected.

"What? Oh, thank you." She tapped her foot and waited for him to address the problem.

"Ok, I will run an ad and hang up a sign on the door," Cade relented.

Cadence looked like she was about to say more, but turned to go instead.

"Cadence, thank you," he called after her.

She stopped and without looking back at him, shrugged and disappeared to the back of the shop. Cade felt like he was separated from reality. All he wanted wanted to know how Cindy was, but he had to get his head together for his business. That night, he decided to do something he hadn't done since he was a teenager. He shaved his beard. He loved his beard, but he needed a change.

Touching the smooth skin that had been covered for years, he stared at his image for a moment. His hair was also getting long. Tomorrow he would visit Hank, who had been cutting his hair for years. When Alex and

Cadence walked into the shop the next morning, their conversation stopped at the sight of Cade's bare naked chin.

"Wow," Cadence said, taken back.

"You look...young." Alex's mouth hung open at the sight.

"Go on, get to work," Cade mock ordered. "I have already received inquiries to the job. I haven't even ran an ad, may not have to."

He turned back to the computer, reviewing the emails with portfolios from the interested candidates. Two of the five were talented and he wondered what their pay requirements would be. Sending emails to each, he set up interviews for the next couple of days and left for Hank's Clippers.

An old blue and red barber pole hung by the front door, and a little bell clanged when he opened it. Hank stood behind a customer, clippers in his hand as he gave the young man a military style buzz cut. They had a base nearby and Cade wondered if the kid was serving. There was a time he had considered joining, but that was years ago. Just before he started living on the streets at seventeen, he had collected information at a school fair from each branch. A man in uniform had visited his foster home. He was with the Navy and had reviewed Cade's test scores for military entrance. They were all required to take the test their senior year. His score was impressive and the recruiter knew it.

Cade's foster father went on a binge that night, Complaining that if Cade up and left before he was eighteen that he wouldn't collect a check on his "sorry ass" anymore. With that, he took his rage out on Cade for the very last time, and Cade fled, preferring the streets to dealing with a drunk every day. His foster mom had been kind, but years of abuse had turned her quiet.

"Hey Cade, it's been a while." Hank's warm smile greeted Cade as he took a seat to wait his turn.

"Hey Hank, how are the grandkids?"

Hank pulled the cape from around the customer he had been working on and brushed off any excess hair. He rung the customer up and wished him well in basic training. Finally, he turned to Cade.

"They are great, Dani is graduating from medical school and Allen is finishing up his doctorate. I would say, they are doing just fine."

He patted the chair, signaling Cade to come have a seat. A picture of Hanks deceased wife sat on the mantle among products, clippers, and combs. She had died several years ago, an aggressive cancer that slowly sapped the life from her. Cade had only asked once about the beautiful woman in the picture and never brought her up to Hank again, unless Hank talked about her, which he usually didn't.

When Cade had been on the streets for almost a year, his hair was filthy and long. He still remembers Hank walking by and stopping in front of him. That day, Hank had motivated Cade to get his act together, or he would die alone and homeless. Hank took Cade into the barber shop and cleaned and cut his hair.

"Now go get a job youngin' and come see me when you need another cut!" Cade could not pay him, but the kind old man just laughed and told him it was on the house. Hank also told him he would have plenty of money with a haircut like that if he would just go apply himself.

Cade still remembers how surprised Tommy was to see him, clean cut and clean shaven. They celebrated after one of Tommy's treatments, and not even two weeks later, Cade had a job at the corner store. He had sent Tommy a text the day before to check in, but they were off on some adventure honeymoon for a few weeks and he never heard back. Tommy's social media sites were full of pictures of them having fun, so he knew he was ok at least.

"I saw you on the news kid," Hank said as he placed the cape around Cade's neck.

"It is a long story Hank."

Cade's heart felt heavy at the mention of the news special. A crazed kidnapper, abducting a young woman and hauling her off to his warehouse of insanity. Many media outlets had covered the story and some were very false in their retelling of what had happened. He had even read an interview between Cindy's parent's and the local news.

"All I got is time. How much are we taking off today?" Hank placed a hand on Cade's shoulder.

"I need a change. I want to be able to brush some back on top, but let's trim the back and maybe take the clippers to the bottom?"

He wasn't sure if that made sense, but he figured Hank would understand. Also, it was just hair, it would grow back. Hank got to work with Cade's hair, but he asked questions about that horrible day and Cade had to relive the whole experience again. When they were finished, Hank removed the cape and brushed off Cade's shoulders.

"Son, it sounds like you are in love with this girl. If you are in love with her, go get her."

He made it sound so easy. Cindy had been traumatized and not to mention her parents hated him. He wasn't sure that it would be so easy. Happy endings in movies never seemed to apply to Cade's life, but he found that he agreed with Hank. Suddenly feeling like he was coming up from his pit of despair, he clasped hands with Hank.

"Thank you Hank. I think you saved me a second time in this life."

A knowing twinkle shown in the old blurry brown eyes that peered at him, and he smiled. Cindy was his girl, and she would always be. He was going to make damn sure of it. Cade placed his helmet on his head, feeling refreshed from the cut and the perspective. Engine purring, he made his way to a fancy condo uptown.

***

Cindy had stayed with her parents for the first few days after her abduction. At first, she didn't mind her mother fretting over her, but then the complaints began and she returned to her condo. She even told her if she had just stayed in medical school, this would never have happened and that she should really call Todd. He had apparently asked about her. Cade had not messaged her, and she was glad for it. That crazy Spencer kid was obsessing over Cade the entire time he had her. His ramblings never made sense, but she was angry at him and Cade for some reason. He had not physically harmed her, but the whole thing had been emotionally distressing. Cindy would never let anyone make her feel so weak again. Lying in bed, she stared at the television.

A shiny bald-headed man flashed a huge smile from the screen, his hands busy slicing fruits and vegetables that he sent through a juicer. After his elaborate demonstration, the shipping and easy payments screen flashed before her. Flipping the channel, Cindy stopped on a locally ran ad. A woman pinned a man to the floor and bent his arm back in a painfully unnatural direction. The same woman from the demonstration gave her testimonial and Cindy jotted down the number to call for her free introductory course.

"Hello, yes I was wanting to come in for the introductory self-defense course. Yes. One hour? Okay, yes. Thank you."

She recognized the warm voice from the petite woman on the screen just moments before. They had an opening in an hour and she considered backing out but decided this was as good a time as any. Looking at her reflection, she was a mess. Her hair was standing out on the sides and her eyes were hollow from sleepless nights. She ran a brush through her hair and dug out her yoga pants and a tank, quickly slipping on her sneakers and running down the stairs.

It was only a few blocks to the gym that they were holding the free course in. She wanted to breathe in the fresh air and stop at the corner shop for a bottle of water. Her mind was busy with thoughts of Cade. She missed him, but she was angry too. She knew she shouldn't blame him for what the maniac had done, but she needed to direct her rage somewhere. Her heart still ached to be with him though. He was the first man to make her feel so confident and safe. That was robbed when Spencer grabbed her outside of her condo and threw her in the back of a van.

Memories of that night flashed through her mind and she stuffed them back down. Stopping in the middle of the sidewalk, she took a deep breath and willed herself to think of something else, anything else. Cade drifted back into her mind. Two passionate nights with him and the handful of dates they had, and yet she felt like she would never be able to love another. Each day without him had been torturous despite the anger that welled deep inside. While she thought it was good that he had given her space, she wondered why he had not attempted to reach out to her, which fueled her anger even further. She picked up her pace and strode into the convenient store.

She had avoided going out in public after her face aired on multiple news outlets for days. Hoping the rest of the world would forget, she was disappointed to find that the clerk behind the counter did recognize her. Bottle of water in hand she stepped up to the counter. An audible inhale from the clerk was the first sign that she was about to be put under the spotlight again.

"You are that girl. The girl from the crazy kidnapping a few weeks back, oh my goodness." Her elderly face was scrunched up in concern and pity.

Cindy just nodded and started to pull out her card when the woman touched her hand.

"Sweetie, this is on me today."

"Thank you."

Surprised that the woman didn't berate her with questions and thankful for her kindness she gave her a genuine smile. She realized it was the first time she had smiled since she had last seen Cade. Her heart beat a little faster at the thought of him and she almost pulled out her phone to text him. Collecting her water bottle and her wits, she left the convenient store and finished her walk to the little gym.

If the instructor recognized her from the news, she didn't act like it. While Maggie was small in stature, her warm voice carried across the room and her demeanor screamed "I am in charge". After they grappled and Maggie showed Cindy a few easy beginners' moves, Cindy knew she was going to sign up for the monthly package. Maggie was also a personal fitness trainer, and Cindy was quickly added to her list of clients. Leaving the gym, muscle aching and a small sweat circling down her back, Cindy felt great for the first time in weeks.

Cindy walked back home and showered. A familiar rumble from the street drew her to the window. Hair dripping and towel wrapped around her midriff, she peered down at Cade's motorcycle and felt her heart jump at the sight of him. She nervously ran her fingers through her hair and ran to her bedroom for something to wear. An old college hoodie and shorts were crumpled up in the corner of her closet that was in complete disarray. She sighed and slipped into the clothes, hoping they were clean. Her doorbell chimed and she made her way down the stairs slowly to her front door.

Blinking at the clean-shaven face and deep green eyes that peered at her, she sucked in a breath at the sight of him. He was handsome with the beard, but without, he was incredible. His hair was brushed back and trimmed in the back with a slight fade at the bottom. Fighting the urge to reach up and run her fingers through his shaggy, clean mane, she folded her hands into fist. They stood in her doorway for what felt like eternity before she collapsed against his chest, breathing him in. His cologne was warm and refreshing.

***

When Cade stepped up to the large navy door, he hesitated only briefly. His nerves making him feel sick, and he took a deep breath as he pushed the little white button that sounded her doorbell. A moment later, Cindy stood before him in a faded hoodie and shorts, her hair still dripping from a recent shower. He was afraid she wouldn't be accepting of his visit. When she collapsed into his chest, he was surprised but happy to have her close again. He kissed her forehead and just held her until she pulled back and they moved into her condo. They moved up the stairs and took a seat around her kitchen table.

"Would you like anything to drink?" She asked him awkwardly and before allowing him to answer, she clanked around in the cabinets and came back a moment later with a glass of wine for each of them.

He sniffed the dark, almost purple, liquid and took a small sip. It was a dry wine that left a film on his tongue. It wasn't his favorite wine he had tasted, but it was also not the worst. Setting his glass back on the table, he looked at Cindy as she took a large sip from her own glass.

"How are you?" He felt silly for asking, but that was the first thing that came out of his mouth.

"I am ok. You?"

"Ok. I have missed you." He looked into those beautiful blue eyes, seeing something behind them he hadn't before.

"I just finished my first self-defense course. It was pretty exciting." She smiled and his heart warmed to see it.

"Good. That is awesome. Where at?"

"A gym just down the street. Maggie Lee runs it. She is a tiny little beast!"

He listened as she told him about her first session. He knew Maggie. She was well known in the community for being a hard-ass, but also a very reputable fitness trainer. He was happy that she was obviously excited about her knew discovery. If it empowered her and filled her with joy, he could easily support it.

"What happened to your beard?" She asked while reaching out and touching his cheek. Her soft hands gently caressed him. He wanted her to keep touching him forever.

"I needed a change," he shrugged.

"I… I like it."

"Hah… well, it has been a long time since my chin was exposed."

"Cade?"

"Yes?"

"I have wanted to ask you something for a long time." She had stopped caressing his cheek and let her hands rest in her lap. Her blue eyes now looking at her hands as she twisted them nervously.

"Ask me anything Cindy."

He took one of her hands in his and rubbed the back of it, trying to sooth her obvious nerves, and calm himself too.

"What happened to your parents?"

Her eyes were back on his. He wondered why of all the questions this was what she wanted to know now. He didn't care though, because he would tell her anything. Time away from her had made him realize just how much he loved her. He loved her. He could honestly say that he was in love with the beautiful woman sitting in front of him, and he couldn't imagine spending his life without her.

"Well, let's see how to begin this. I can still remember the small run-down apartment that we lived in. I believe it was an apartment anyway. Up on the east end, the poor side of the city. I am not even sure how I survived past infancy. My parents sold and used drugs. Anyways, when I was four, I went to the kitchen to make myself a sandwich. I have a picture of when I was that age, I was a scrawny little thing. I probably only ate junk, or whatever I could find in the kitchen. But, I came back from the kitchen with my sandwich and found my mom and dad sitting on that old broken down couch in the middle of the room. Springs poked out and stuffing had given way to a sagging heap of fabric."

He paused and checked to see if she was still following. Her eyes were filled with sadness, not pity, but sadness for what was to come.

"They sat there, motionless. I am not sure how long they had been that way, I had been playing with some toy or another and had just decided to get a sandwich. They were usually quiet, and they always told me to stay quiet too, so it wasn't anything new. This wasn't the first time I had found them passed out, but I knew this time was different. Their eyes were open and blank. I put my sandwich down and walked over to them, and just stared. Neither one was breathing. How could I have known at four, I don't know, but I did."

Cindy was covering her mouth now and one single tear rolled down her cheek.

"They were known to overdose, so I was aware of how to call 911. Within minutes, the ambulance had pulled in and everything happened quickly. They laid my parents flat and tried to bring them back, but they were both gone. I watched as the EMT's pulled the needles and tourniquets from their arms and zipped them in the black bags. The next day I was taken into custody, but they found out that my aunt was my closest kin and they placed me in her care… to her disappointment."

Cindy reached out and placed her hand on his arm. He felt her squeeze as he looked at a blank space on the wall. Years of suppressed memories flooding out of him, as if a dam had been broken within.

"My aunt had a job that required a lot of travel. When she saw how self-sufficient I was, she left me at home alone. When I was old enough to go to school, I walked to and from the bus stop and took care of myself. It took them, the state, three years to find out that I was taking care of myself. I had a fever at school and when they couldn't reach my aunt, I told them that she was in some other state on business. Once again, I was hustled into custody by the state and before I knew it I was in and out of foster homes. My last foster home seemed promising in the beginning. I was thirteen and had been acting out recently. My foster mom was sweet, but she was very quiet when her husband came home. It didn't take long until I figured out the source of her quietness and the rage behind that sat behind a constant empty bottle. By seventeen I was tired of the abuse. I left and took to the streets where I met Tommy."

He stopped. He had not shared this much about himself with anyone before. It felt good to get it all off his chest, but he was afraid of how she would respond or react to his admission. Cade looked at those blue eyes as they pierced through him. Something other than sadness was there, anger.

"I was never abused or witnessed the death of a family member," Cindy explained. "But I felt trapped by my family's name and ambitions. I still do."

He loved that she wanted to relate to him somehow. He couldn't imagine growing up in that miniature castle. Her parents did seem verbally and emotionally abusive in a way, and he had always thought that was worse than a punch to the gut. If his foster father had tried to break him, he did a poor job with his fists. If he had tried using his words to break him, he might have been more successful.

"They are a bit high-strung. I am sure they mean well," Cade tried to reason. He wasn't sure if he believed that, but he thought it was appropriate to say.

"Thank you, but they are overbearing and controlling. I am so sorry for how our dinner went. They should not have treated you that way. They don't know you."

"I love you." Before he could stop himself, the words just spilled out.

"Huh?" Her eyebrows shot up and he suddenly felt that same sick feeling in the pit of his stomach.

"I love you Cindy Watkins."

He wanted to say more, but he felt stupid. His brain and mouth couldn't work and he wanted to hold her close.

"I...I. I love you too."

Her face was twisted with confusion, but she had said the same three words and his heart skipped a beat.

The pair sat quietly for a moment, sharing the moment when it was shattered by Cindy's doorbell ringing. They both jumped at the sound. She walked over to her balcony window and looked down below. Whoever it was, she sighed and walked down the stairs. A moment later, he heard another male voice. It was pompous and arrogant. His skin crawled at the absurdity of it and he walked to the stairs and peered down. That same smug doctor from her hospital, stood in her doorway with a large bouquet of roses. A teddy bear poked out from under his arm and Cade thought he would vomit.

"Hello Todd," Cindy sneered.

"Hey beautiful."

That made Cade clinch his hand. *That guy deserves a fist to his narcissistic face.*

"I can't really talk right now Todd," Cindy tried to evade.

Her face looked almost as disgusted as Cade's as she looked at the teddy bear in the crook of Todd's arm.

"I just wanted to bring these by and check on you. I have missed you at work."

"What, nobody to change the bedpans?"

Cade remembered her mumbling that at the dinner table and wondered about the story behind it. Either way, he decided to join her and was glad he had, because the look on Todd's face when he noticed him walking down the steps was priceless.

"You. You cleaned that fuzz dog off your face I see," Todd tried to insult.

Cade narrowed his eyes and smirked.

"I had a dog on my face? Surprised I missed that. Sounds terribly uncomfortable."

He heard Cindy suck in air as she tried not to laugh beside him.

"Well, I brought you these flowers and this teddy bear. You still have my number. Your parents told me to come get you this Saturday at seven-o-clock for a family dinner on their estate."

"Those dinners are pretty eventful," Cade chimed in. "Are you sure you can handle that in your busy doctor schedule?"

"At least I can pay my rent. What do you even do, covered in all of that filth and allowing your beard to grow to Neanderthal standard?"

"Oh, you know, mooch off beautiful and wealthy young ladies."

He placed his hand on the small of Cindy's back and felt her body tremble, suppressing the laughter that threatened to bubble out. Todd stood with his mouth gaping at Cade's words. He wasn't sure if Todd was that dense to believe him or if he sensed the sarcasm. Todd huffed, placed the flowers and teddy bear in Cindy's arms, and turned to leave. As soon as he had stomped away down the steps to his car, Cindy and Cade fell into a fit of laughter.

"I really wish he had brought you chocolate. At least I could have had something sweet out of it." Looking at each other, they fell into another bout of laughter.

"Dinner with him and my parents? I feel like its the medieval era and they are trying to force me into a loveless marriage."

She wiped the laughter tears out of her eyes and looked at Cade. Marriage. He hadn't even thought about that yet, but he could see her ten, twenty, even thirty years down the road by his side. His serious face must have worried her, because she furrowed her brow in concern.

"Cade?" She prodded.

"Sorry, I was just thinking about his face when I tag along to this dinner."

"I think you should sit this one out. I am going to find a way to dissuade them from their fantasy that Todd is the perfect match for me and bring them on board with the idea of us being an us."

She squeezed his arm and moved in to rest her head on his chest and wrap her arms around him. Every time they touched it felt right, like she was his puzzle piece that he had been missing his whole life.

"You, had better leave," she whispered and tilted up to look at him.

Cade bent down to kiss her softly; their first kiss since the incident. He felt her melt in his arms and while he was turned on by their proximity, he wasn't going to press for anything more tonight. She was clearly not ready for them to make love yet. He was just happy to even hold her. Kissing was just a bonus. They broke from their kiss, but not their embrace.

"Have you already returned to work?" He held her another minute longer. She shook her head in response to his question.

"No, they have let me take extra leave. I think I am ready to get back to the mayhem though. I miss the chaos and routine."

He frowned when she said chaos, but he didn't say anything. If that was her comfort zone, who was he to say otherwise. His own situation at the shop was stressing him enough as it is. Which reminded him, he had interviews to prepare for.

"Ok, I will go for tonight. I have to interview some potentially new artists at the shop this week. You should stop by and see where I work sometime."

He finally let go of her and stepped towards her front door.

"I would like that."

She smiled and he had to force himself not to go over and kiss those perfect pink lips one more time. Cade walked through the door and down to his bike. He straddled her and started the engine. His helmet back on his head, he looked up at the balcony and saw Cindy staring down at him. Her smile was warm and she blew him a kiss. Normally that would have seemed absurd to him, but he found her blowing him a kiss to be somehow sultry and seductive.

When he made it back into his apartment, he placed his coat and keys in the usual spot and looked around his apartment. Days spent moping around had left his place a total wreck. Feeling good after sharing his story with the love of his life and having her accept him motivated him to clean the place. When he had finished throwing out the last bag of trash, he looked up at the full moon shining down on him. Stars twinkled against the dark night sky, and he saw a shooting star race across the vastness.

Maybe his luck would improve now. He wasn't much for superstition, but he was hopeful.

11

At the shop the next day, his first interviewee was running late. Not the best first impression, but as an artist, he understood the problems with procrastination. His phone buzzed and he opened an attachment from Cindy. If she was trying to drive him mad, she was doing a fantastic job of it. In the picture, she stood in front of a dressing room mirror wearing a simple floral dress that fell below her knees. The next one, she wore an orange loose fitted dress that looked like an oversize shirt that buttoned up all the way and a brown leather belt rested on her waist. A text message then accompanied the pictures.

Hey. Which one do you like better?
The floral one. He responded.
Awesome.

A moment later, his phone buzzed again and he opened the image only to fumble and drop the phone in his lap. Looking around to make sure nobody else had seen, he scrolled back to the image. She stood in front of that same mirror, one arm hooked under her breasts in a sexy pose as the other took the picture. His eyes traveled down the length of her naked body, resting on her wide hips that curved in the perfect hour glass figure. Black boy shorts rested below her hips, just outlining that sweet spot he wanted to bury himself in again. Feeling himself grow hard, he texted her back.

Evil woman.

She sent some smiley face text at him and he groaned. Thoughts of what he would do if he was in that dressing room with her raced through his mind. Just then, the bell over the door rang and a young man with spiked hair walked through the door.

"Hello, can I help you?" Cade already knew this was most likely his first interviewee.

"I am here for an interview," the young man asked nervously.

"Awesome, Jackson?"

Cade stuck out his hand and the young man gripped it in a strong shake.

"Yes sir."

Ouch. Being called sir made him feel old. *Maybe the kid is trying to make a good impression since he is running late.*

"Let's head to the back of the shop and we can go over your portfolio."

Thirty minutes later, he ushered Jackson out of the shop and shook his head. His pay expectations were ridiculous and his attitude was even more so. Cade tried hard to not pass too much judgment on the kid, since he was so young, but he was too damn cocky. His next scheduled interview was in an hour.

"How did it go boss?" Cadence swung into his office, bouncing on her feet.

"Are you ok today?" Cade asked, concerned at her unusual bubblyness.

He looked up at her and saw her face beaming. Her hair was now a rainbow of colors.

"Perfectly peachy," she responded.

Just then, the light bounced off a glittering object on her ring finger.

"Cadence?"

"Yes boss?" She was practically glowing. He had never seen her this elated, or even this emotional.

"What's on your finger?" He cocked an eyebrow as she blushed and looked at her hand quickly.

"Uh, well, Alex asked me to marry him last night and I said yes."

"Congratulations. That is wonderful news!" Cade's face stretched into a large smile and he stood up to kiss Cadence on the cheek.

"Thank you." Her blush was spreading.

"Well, go get some work done."

She smiled and turned to greet the next customer. He made his way back to Alex's little office.

"Hey man, congratulations," Cade said, stretching his hand out.

For the first time in all of the years he had known Alex, a big smile spread across his face. Alex's hand met Cade's and Cade pulled him in close.

"Thanks man," Alex said.

"You're welcome. You two are perfect and I am genuinely happy for you both."

"Awesome. I think she was a little worried how you would react. I told her you would be fine. Women... right?"

"Well, I guess I need to hire someone quick. Before you two elope and run away to Europe," Cade Joked.

He shook Alex's hand and turned back to check if his next interview was there yet.

"Nah, we are just going to rent a cabin in the mountains a few hours north. We would love to go outside of the country, but we just want to get away from the city for a few days."

Cade looked back at Alex. He was truly happy for his friends and coworkers. They had found love and a new chapter in their life was beginning. When did he get so sappy? Clearly, when he fell in love himself.

After a terrible interview, his next one went well and he hired her on the spot. The next two were equally wonderful and he decided to hire both as well. Two more tattoo artists and one more body modification artist. They were going to need to expand, because there weren't enough rooms for all of them. Cade had the money now since his business was going so well. He would have to start looking at property so they could move as soon as possible.

While he was distracted flipping through properties, the bell over his door rang and a to go cup of coffee was placed in front of him. Looking up, he was surprised to see those beautiful blues looking at him.

"Hey," Cade gushed through a smile.

"Hey, brought you coffee."

Cindy looked around the lobby of his shop and Cade moved to join her. Feeling a sense of pride as she looked around at his creation, he wanted to take her on a tour. She followed him down the hall and he showed her the rooms they had set up for customers and their offices in the back. Cadence was sitting in a chair beside Alex, looking at their schedule when he walked in with Cindy.

"Hey guys. I want you to meet someone."

They looked up and Cadence's mouth dropped as she recognized Cindy from the news. Not saying anything, she quickly closed her mouth and smiled, standing to shake Cindy's hand.

"Nice to meet you," Cindy said with a smile.

Alex said as he stayed in his seat. "Hello."

Alex was not one for small talk most days. Cade was glad he at least said something more than a grunt.

"It is nice to meet you both. I love the shop. Your hair is awesome." She looked at Cadence and cocked her head to the side, taking in the array of colors that covered her head.

"Thanks." Cadence absently touched her hair and then looked at Alex.

"Want a piercing?" Cade said jokingly but Cindy's eyes lit up at the idea.

"Actually, yes."

He was surprised but he would do anything she asked. He took a moment to stumble for the next works.

"Well, uh… we could make that happen."

He looked to Cadence, who shrugged her shoulders up and pointed at the schedule. Seeing the look on Cade's face, she put the schedule down.

"You know what goldilocks," Cadence mocked. "Let's do this."

Cade rolled his eyes at her abrupt nature, but he knew how she could be. Cindy had a polite and nervous smile, and Cade knew he would have to say something about that exchange later. As it turns out, he didn't have to say anything. When they had finished, Cadence and Cindy were hooked arm in arm and laughing. Their stark difference in appearance stopping Cade in his tracks. Despite this, they seemed like the best of friends. He searched for her piercing, but didn't see anything visible. She pulled up her shirt and revealed a freshly pierced belly button. The skin was raised and pink around the new barbell that ran through the skin on the top half of her navel.

"Do you like it?" Cade inquired.

She nodded and then hugged Cadence. He didn't even know that Cadence allowed anyone to do that, but she hugged Cindy back. When Cindy wasn't looking, Cadence mouthed that she liked her to Cade and gave him an enthusiastic thumbs-up.

"Now… do you like it?" Cindy played with the piercing while staring at Cade.

They were standing in the lobby and she had moved close. Her breath tickling his ear as she purred into it. Feeling himself melt, he nodded and he pulled her in close. He pressed himself against her, hoping she could feel just how much he liked it. When he looked at her eyes they were liquid pools, filled with lust. Taking advantage of teasing her for earlier, he leaned in and kissed her slowly but also passionately, making his intentions clear. Lightly, he cupped one of her breast in his hand and just barely brushed his thumb over the top of her now raised nipple. Moaning into his mouth, he smiled and pulled away from her. Dazed from the moment, she stood there and looked at him longingly.

"I am going to take you on a proper date after you break yourself away from this dinner with your family and Todd."

He spat the name out as if he had tasted something sour. He did not like the man and he was not liking the idea of her having dinner with him at her parents but he wouldn't interfere, yet. He trusted her and her judgment on the matter. Seeing the jealousy in his eyes, she just shook her head and laughed.

"I can't wait."

With that, she left and he suddenly realized how much his teasing her had affected him. His pants were uncomfortable and he had to shift himself to try and hide it.

12

Saturday came too quickly and Cindy went out of her way to dress as unappealing as possible. She hoped that Cade would hold up his end of the deal and not interfere. If she was ever going to hopefully make her family see reason, she needed him to not show up at their door cursing the "saint" Todd; the pompous idiot. She couldn't believe she ever went out with him in the first place. They didn't last long, but it was long enough for her mother to catch wind of it and soon she tried planning a wedding that would never happen.

While she would have preferred comfy sweats and a t-shirt, she still wore a simple, but modest dress to appease her mother. Todd was at her door ten minutes till seven. Rolling her eyes, she looked at the huge bouquet of roses he brought her again. Trying not to vomit, she took them from him and sat them next to the now drooped and dying ones from a few days back. She relished in the fact that he noticed the old ones hadn't been tended too. It made her feel a little bad, but he had it coming. He knew she was with Cade, but he insisted on entertaining this horrid idea of her parents. With everything they had done for her after her kidnapping, she would give them this. After, she would make sure they knew she was an adult, learning to defend herself, and that Todd was never going to happen.

"You look, beautiful." His face was scrunched up as he analyzed her modest dress and he hesitated before adding beautiful.

Despite her efforts, she felt his eyes were still all over her body. It made her sick and ready to run back into her condo and cancel the whole thing.

"Thanks," she managed to respond.

She saw him staring at her as if he wanted her to praise him on his looks. He was wearing an expensive fitted suit and he had put gel or a styling product in his short hair to make it stand up in the front. While he may have been going for something attractive, it made her want to giggle. Pulling up to her parent's estate, she held back a groan as she saw her parents elegantly dressed for the occasion. Now her mother would surely have a fit over her outfit. Surprisingly, she didn't. As a matter of fact, her parents were overly nice during the whole affair.

"Hello sweetie," her mother cooed as she wrapped her in a tight hug that was awkward from lack of practice.

Her shoulders shrugged up and she shot her brows up in question at her mother's behavior. Once inside, Cindy saw a decanter in the middle of the table, half empty. They each took their seat around the dinner table and she felt her phone buzz in her lap. Looking down, the screen lit up with Cade's number.

Hey beautiful. I can still rescue you?

Smiling she swiped the screen to respond.

I am good for now. Mom is drunk. Wish you were here.

I love you.

That was the second time he had told her he loved her. Her heart fluttered wildly in her chest. She rested her finger over the text box to respond and hesitated. She knew she was in love with this man, so why was she sitting at this awful dinner with her family and that sneering, good for nothing Todd? Her mother was fussing over his suit and flirting with him, while her indifferent father picked at the meal on his plate. Feeling disgusted by her mother's display, she looked back at her phone and quickly swiped the three words back to Cade. After this was all over, she would need to spend some time with him, because his little fondling at the shop the other day had left her frustrated for days.

"Cindy, hello, Cindy, what on earth are you fiddling with?" Her mother was glaring at her.

"The food looks good. Did you hire a new cook?"

Her mother's eyebrows shot up and a drunken blush rested on her cheeks. It was a comical face really, that made Cindy cough as she tried to take a sip of her wine. Her mother ignored her and turned back to Todd, that smile returning to her face.

"I hear you are considering your very own practice in the city?" She fluttered her eyelashes at him. If he realized her flirtation, he didn't let on.

"Yes. I believe we need a good family practice, and I could use a break from the strain of the emergency room."

He feigned exhaustion. As if he had to change a patient's lines, suction them, and clean their bedpans, turn them to make sure they didn't develop bed sores, and so much more that ran through her head. Her never ending list of things she had to monitor and do was exhausting. Sure, she knew some excellent doctors, who did far more than their peers, but Todd was not one of them.

"Isn't that lovely Cindy?" Her mother waited for her to respond.

"Oh yes, truly," she mocked.

When they had finally finished their dinner, Cindy's father retired to his study and her mother continued to probe Todd on the latest news and gossip. Listening to him talk to her mother, she couldn't believe just how full of himself he was. Every answer ended with something about him. Suddenly, her mother stood up, stretched and placed a hand on Todd's shoulder.

"Well, thank you Todd for gracing us with your splendid company. I do hope that you will be returning again soon."

She leaned down to kissed him on the cheek for far too long. Swallowing to avoid gagging, Cindy stood to leave as well. Picking up the now empty decanter, her mother walked to the liquor cabinet and sat it inside, while also grabbing out another bottle and glass. She left them alone in the dining room.

"Well, that was delicious. Let's get going shall we?" Todd suggested.

They escorted themselves out of the estate and back to his little sports car. Her mother was looking down from a window, not at her, but at Todd as they slid into their seats. He had already jumped into his and started the engine.

Such a gentleman she thought as she opened her door and sat down.

As they headed back towards the city, she felt relieved that the night would be over soon and she would make sure that Todd understood there was nothing between them. When he turned away from her condo, she felt a sudden nervous jolt shoot through her.

"Um, Todd, my condo is back that way?"

"I know, but I am taking you back to my place. I thought we could have a nightcap before you head home."

"Todd, I really just want to go home and go to bed."

Ignoring her, he continued down the street. When the car stopped at a red light, she felt herself kick into survival mode and she bolted out the door of his still car. She heard him calling out to her, but she ignored him and started hiking back towards her condo. His car rumbled and he turned back to chase her up the street.

"Come on Cindy. Just get in the car," he begged.

"No Todd. I will not be forced to spend another moment with you. You're a slimy bastard."

"And you're a stupid bitch. I can take care of you, that street rat cannot."

His eyes were narrowed and she turned at him. Anger was rippling through her as she stomped across the street to his driver's side window. A smile spread across his face as he thought she was actually going to rejoin him in his sick fantasy. Instead, she balled her hand into a fist and slammed it right into his nose. Pain radiated up into her wrist and she was certain she had just broken her thumb or one of the metacarpals in her hand. As the blood seeped from his nose and he held himself in pain, she felt great. It took him a few minutes to shake himself from the pain, and a line of cars had formed behind him, honking despite the time of night.

Not able to decipher the curse words that he mumbled under his breath, she stormed off before one of the cars decided to fly around him and possibly hit her too. On the sidewalk, she held her hand to her chest, pain throbbing up and down her arm. Using her left hand to call Cade, she tried to steady her voice. She didn't need to send him into full panic.

"Hello?" His voice sounded wide awake, despite the hour.

"Hey, you're still awake?"

"Of course, I was waiting to hear about the dinner."

"Could you come pick me up?"

"Where are you?" She heard his voice change pitch and knew that she had alarmed him.

"Um, Franklin Avenue."

"On my way, stay put and please be careful. Keep your phone in your hand," he ordered.

She heard him slam a door and within seconds she heard his bike scream to life. She hung up and kept her phone out just in case. It felt like forever before she heard him coming down the street, when in fact it had only been minutes. He pulled up and jumped off his bike, almost dropping it to the ground.

"Come on, let's get you home," he urged.

"Um, actually, the emergency room would be best."

He stopped and turned to her, anger flashing behind those penetrating green eyes. He started looking her over, checking for any physical signs that she was hurt.

"What did he do? Did he hurt you? I will kill him."

She snorted and chuckled, but the shaking hurt her hand. His eyes rested on her face and he looked confused.

"I am sorry. It's just. I hurt myself. I sort of punched him in the nose. Pretty sure it is broken like something in my hand."

Anger quickly fading from those beautiful green eyes, she saw both humor and concern flood into them.

"You punched him in the nose?" Before she could answer, he kissed her and smiled. "That's fantastic! I wish I had seen it, but let's go get that hand taken care of."

He walked with his arm around her to the bike and they sped off toward the hospital.

***

At first Cade was furious. He was ready to rip that smug face off of Todd's little cocky head, but when Cindy told him she had punched him in the nose, he had to refrain from doubling over in laughter. While he would have preferred being the one to have landed the punch, mostly because he knows how to not break his bones, he was happy to see her standing up for herself. When they pulled up to her work, he wrapped his arm around her and they walked in.

It was busy at this hour, but her coworkers stopped to stare at her walk through the doors with this tattoo covered man. Feeling their eyes burn into him with accusations, he thought to himself, *great, they think I hurt her.*

"What did you do sugar?" A woman with gold rimmed glasses stormed towards them.

"Hey Annie, it's not as bad as it looks."

Before she could say anything, Annie put her index finger in Cade's chest and looked him square in the eyes.

"If you had anything to do with this, I will wipe the floor with your handsome face."

Cade chucked, he liked this woman.

"Annie, I broke my hand punching Todd in the face after I was forced to have dinner with him at my parents. Which is ridiculous that I was forced to do so, but if you only knew my parents."

Annie stopped, her face shifting from angry mother hen to something else. Cade wasn't sure, and then the woman bent forward and a loud rattling came from her. He didn't realize the woman, who had clearly smoked her entire life, was in stitches. She bent back up, her face covered in a grin from ear to ear.

"Oh, so that's what happened to the princess's nose! Boy, I wish I had seen it! He came in here with that black n' blue lookin' lump in the middle of his face, and when I asked him what he did, he just growled and stomped off! Forced to have dinner with your parents? Girl, tell em' no!"

"I told her I wish I had seen her punch him too," Cade added. He was smiling but a quick sharp glance from Annie told him she didn't trust him yet.

"Let's go take a look at it," Annie urged.

Cade began to follow them back, but Annie's large hand held out to him.

"Annie, it's ok."

"No it isn't. He may be good lookin' and all, but he'll have to wait in the lobby like the rest of em'."

It irked Cade that he couldn't join her, but he wasn't about to tell the lady no.

"It's ok, I will wait for you," Cade assured her.

Cindy's blue eyes shown with admiration as she was escorted back by the clucking Ms. Annie, and he took a seat in the hospital lobby.

After about fifteen minutes and a can of soda later, he started pacing the floor. Late night infomercials danced across the television and he tried to find something interesting from them, but he wasn't interested in a super blender or a tool with twenty possible uses. He wanted to know how his girl was. When the clock reflected an hour had passed, he stood up to walk towards the front desk, but Annie and Cindy came walking around the corner. Cindy's wrist was wrapped in a colorful cast. She stepped up to him and kissed him on the cheek.

"Annie, let me introduce you to Cade."

Annie's eyes narrowed only slightly, something hidden behind those dark eyes.

"Nice to meet you Cade," Annie managed.

"Nice to meet you Ms. Annie."

He reached out to take one of her large hands in his, and she yanked him in close. She was strong, which was shocking.

"If you harm my girl here, I know just the right medicinal concoction to make you think your peter has fallen off!"

The woman's threats only increased Cade's admiration.

"I will keep that in mind," he chuckled.

"You be sure you do."

"Oh Annie, stop it," Cindy protested. "Have a good night."

She wrapped her arms around Annie in a hug and the old woman pointed a threatening finger at Cade. It was all he could do not to laugh, but he was glad to see someone caring for Cindy the way Annie did. Nodding his head he understood, he took his coat and wrapped it around Cindy as they made their way outside. Once on his bike, Cindy could only hold him with one arm, but she held on tight. He loved having her so close, knowing she was safe. When he got to her condo, he walked her to her door.

"Oh, I am so tired," Cindy complained.

"Go get some rest beautiful, you had an eventful night."

When he turned to leave she reached out with her good hand and grabbed him.

"Cade, do you mind just holding me tonight?"

"Of course not."

He followed her up into her condo and for the first time in years, he crawled into bed fully clothed. Spooning the love of his life, he held her close and knew this was where he should always be. When her soft snores floated up and over to him, he kissed her hair softly and breathed her in deep. He loved her scent and warmth. When he woke up the next morning, he couldn't think of a time he slept better than last night. Well, he could think of a couple times he had slept well, and they were both with her.

What had woke him up was Cindy's body pressing into his. She was stretching and her body that curved perfectly into his was pressing against his early morning arousal. Groaning from the desire that stirred within him, he resisted ripping her clothes off and making love to her.

"Cade?" Her morning voice was warm and husky.

"Good morning," he whispered.

She turned toward him and kept her hurt hand at her side.

"Good morning," she responded with a smile.

He leaned over and kissed her nose.

"Want some breakfast?"

"Mmm, among other things," she purred.

Her eyes flashed down to his arousal and then returned to his own. He kissed her and caressed her arm, little goose bumps rising where he touched and she moaned into the kiss.

Her phone shrilled on the table by her bed, causing them both to jump. Groaning, she leaned over him and saw her mother's number on the screen. Hitting the ignore button she rolled back on top of Cade, kissing him, trying to avoid hitting either of them with her cast. Her phone buzzed again and she growled as she grabbed it up and answered.

"Yes mother?"

"I'm outside," she crooned from the speaker. "I see a big black piece of death on two wheels out here. I didn't want to come up to another naked fest like last time."

"I will meet you at the door."

She hung up and sighed. They looked at each other longingly and rolled out of bed.

"Should I sneak out a back window?" Grinning, he followed her down the stairs.

"She has already seen your bike," Cindy reminded him.

When she opened the door, Cade stayed back as her mother breezed through the door. She held her purse in her hand and kept her body stiff.

"I see Todd isn't here and...what happened to your hand!" Her eyes bulged and she turned on Cade. "I knew you were no good. I knew it! I will call the police!"

As she started rummaging through her purse, Cindy grew enraged.

"Mother, stop, NOW!"

Cindy's voice carried throughout the entire condo and her mother stood shocked. Her tight lips split and her mouth dropped, surprised at the tone in which Cindy used with her.

"I punched Todd in the nose when he tried to take me to his place last night, and wouldn't take no for an answer. He is disgusting, lude, and a womanizer mother! I am in love with Cade, and since I am a grown woman and this is my house. I suggest you leave."

As if her mother hadn't heard any of the last part, she stared mouth still gaping at her daughter.

"You, punched Todd?" She asked.

"Mother, he wasn't taking no for an answer, so yes, I punched him."

"Well, I…" She huffed up her chest and seemed to process the entire thing. "Wait…he tried to force you to go with him? You punched him, and you are in love with Cade?"

Her mother started fanning herself, lost in thought.

"Yes, I am in love with Cade."

She turned towards him and her blue eyes beamed at him, sending waves of excitement through him. Cindy's mother hooked her by the arm and moved into the next room. She may have been trying to be discreet, but Cade heard every word.

"Are you happy dear?" Cindy's mother asked.

"What, you have never asked me that before."

"Are you, happy?" She repeated.

"Very." Cindy smiled.

"Well, I will talk to your father and we will have to have lunch with you both. If he makes you happy, I will try to look past his…physical mutilations on his arms and try to be accepting."

"Uh, ok," Cindy stammered. "Thank you?"

"I love you sweetie. I have never been very good at this whole thing, but I love you."

"I love you too mom."

Cade peaked around the corner and saw them hugging. Cindy's face was scrunched in confusion at her mother's behavior as she shrugged at him.

"Now go take a shower, you stink. And you," Cindy's mother turned to Cade. "Stop peaking around the corner and come in here."

Cade wondered how she knew he was peaking, but stepped in awkwardly.

"Do you have something nice to wear this time?" Her mother had tilted her head back, chin held high as she inspected him.

"I can find something."

"Good, make sure you do."

She tapped him on the chest and that was the second time this week a mother hen had poked him.

"Yes ma'am."

"Hmm. And please do where something a little more flattering this time Cindy, that dress is awful! Also, you are all frumpy today, did you sleep in it?"

"I will talk to you later mother." She ushered her mother towards the door.

Cade stepped up and wrapped his arms around her.

"Do I stink?" Cindy asked, trying to check herself.

"Not to me."

"I am going to go take a shower. I guess I need to wrap this in plastic or something." She held out her bulging casted hand.

"Do you need any help?"

Passion and lust entering his voice as he moved his hands down her front and pulled up on her dress, causing her to tremble against him. She pulled away after a moment.

"No, you go," she objected, with hesitation. "I have to go by the hospital and see what they have me scheduled for this week."

They held hands and he leaned down for one more kiss.

"I should stop by the shop. I feel like my staff thinks I have quit on them. Oh, I forgot to tell you, we have to expand. What time is it anyway, crap! I am supposed to be downtown looking at a potential new location. I will call you later."

With that he moved to leave. His lust unsatisfied for now, but he would have to take care of that later. Cindy waved down at him from her balcony and he waved back.

13

Zooming down the street, he made it to the address the realtor had given him and checked his phone. He was only five minutes late, but she was tapping her foot by the street corner. He noticed her attitude change when he peeled off his helmet. The next thirty minutes he had to politely dissuade the woman from leaving him her personal phone number, but she still managed to slip it on the back of the business card she handed him. She brushed his fingers with her own and smiled at him.

Ignoring her advances, Cade left her and the ridiculously overpriced building behind. He wasn't sure where they would move the shop to, but the property his realtor had shown him was outrageous. Returning to his own shop, he found Alex, Cadence, and the new hires lounging in the lobby.

"Hey guys," Cade greeted.

Cadence jumped up first.

"How was it?" She asked.

He had to think for a second, and realized she meant the building.

"It was nice, but too expensive. I have a few more locations to look at this week. Did you want to tag along?"

He didn't even think to invite her the first time, but he could see she was dying to evaluate the places herself.

"Yes, please!" She practically jumped at the idea.

Cade narrowed his eyes at his employee, unsure of her still unusual behavior.

"Are you ok Cadence?" Cade asked, glancing at her with unsure eyes.

Her eyes darted to Alex.

"Well, we have some more news..." Cadence teased. Alex stood up this time and put his arm around Cadence. "We are pregnant."

Cade was floored. That was wonderful news, but it still shocked him. He didn't even think Cadence liked children, but the excitement in their faces chased any doubts from his mind.

"Well damn. Congratulations guys! That is wonderful news! Engaged, expecting a baby, what next?"

Cadence hugged him and then moved over to Alex who had returned to his burrito. Her joy from a moment ago was replaced with a look of pure disgust and she covered her mouth and ran to the back.

"They say if you have a lot of morning sickness you are probably having a girl," Alex said between bites and smiled.

Cade's two new hires looked bored and he viewed the schedule. They were booked tight that afternoon and evening, so that would hopefully satisfy them. Cade wondered how Cindy was doing at the hospital and hoped she didn't run into Todd while she was there. He clinched his fists, still itching to punch him. He had to stifle his anger earlier when Cindy had explained the whole story to her mother.

"You ok there buddy?" Cadence walked back through looking at his fists.

"Huh, yes. I am good."

Cade relaxed and checked his email for any new requests. An invitation to a well-known event in the city flashed in his inbox. Usually people dressed as their favorite fictional characters and many vendors had to register early for a spot.

"Cadence?"

"Hmm," she replied.

"Did you have anything to do with this?"

She peered over his shoulder at the email.

"Oh, yes. Yes I did. Yay!"

"Well, I suppose you can handle the shop and the new hires while Alex and I head to this next week."

She slugged him in the shoulder and he threw up his hands in mock defeat. He knew she would kill him if he didn't take her with him.

"I am kidding!" Cade confessed.

Cadence narrowed her eyes at him and brandished a playful fist. "Better be."

***

Cindy walked through the automatic doors at the hospital and made her way to the nurse's station. Her hours had changed, and she was no longer on the graveyard shift. Normally she would be upset she wasn't asked, but this meant she could actually be on a normal schedule for a while. She was distracted when Todd approached the desk. She felt eyes on her and jumped when she saw how close he stood.

"Shit," she gasped and held her broken hand to her chest.

"Hi." His voice was gruff his nose was swollen.

Green and yellow bruising sprouted out on each side. She could faintly see that the bridge was a little crooked and felt some satisfaction and an ache in her broken hand. A dull ache radiated in her wrist at the same time and she remembered it was time for another round of pain meds. Maybe that was karma for feeling so smug that his nose was also broken.

"Hello Todd."

"I just want to say, I am sorry."

She wasn't sure how sincere he was, because it seemed to her that he had difficulty just spitting those simple three words out. Either way, she wasn't going to pry. He didn't wait for her to respond; he just turned on his heel and walked away.

"Mmm mm mmm." Annie walked behind the counter.

"Annie, do you ever go home?" Cindy chuckled.

"Every other Sunday."

Humor twinkled in her dark eyes and Cindy wondered if there was any truth behind it. She felt like no matter what time of day, Annie was here.

"Seriously, you are always here!"

"Honey child, when you have two options to choose from, you choose the more excitin' one. If I went home, I might find a good sitcom or maybe I would crochet a scarf. Bah! I would rather be here watchin' this real life soap opera unfold. Our patients keep me entertained and your drama is enough to write to one of those daytime television hosts about. Now, I might go home to watch that if you were on it with these fellas."

"You are finding way too much humor with my despair."

"Despair? Girl, you have two good lookin' men fightin' over you. Of course, Dr. Panmsy Mamsy doesn't need your affections, but this solid biker dude, now that is awesome! Write me a book or a juicy blog about you two, that would be fabulous! I doubt I could put it down for days. You have been kidnapped, sorry to bring that up, then forced to dine with the enemy and your family, and then you punched the man in the face! I just need a soda machine and some popcorn."

"Oh Annie."

She shook her head but laughed. Her life had been pretty interesting since she met Cade at Tommy and Heather's wedding. At the thought of her best friend, Cindy realized she needed to check in on Heather, she hadn't spoken with her in over a week, which wasn't normal. She looked through her messages, just to make sure she hadn't missed any and there they were. Heather had sent her messages, but they were apparently on their honeymoon. Pictures from their adventures flooded across her screen and she smiled. It looked like they were having a wonderful time. She thought about going on a honeymoon with Cade and stopped herself.

"Honey, what is it? Was it something I said?" Those big bushy eyebrows were laced with concern as she began to evaluate Cindy.

"I just realized, I am so in love with the guy I could marry him. If he asked me, I would say yes. Who does that Annie? We haven't been together long enough to know that yet! Have we?"

"Honey, I am not the best at relationships, obviously, but I think if love is going to find you it will find you when it damn well pleases."

She took Cindy's good hand in hers and squeezed. Her hands were large and warm as they enclosed around her own.

"It is just so crazy Annie, when I am with him, I feel so free to be myself. And let's not even start on the sex. Wow, it is amazing. I am not an expert in bed, but oh it is awesome."

"Well, that's good. You definitely need to test drive before you purchase." She winked and Cindy laughed so hard she cried a little.

"Ok, I need to get going. They have me on mornings now, so I need to go try and rotate my schedule. I also have a date with my personal trainer. I took up self-defense classes, you would be proud."

"Oh, sug', I am proud. Every woman should be able to protect herself without a man. That is why I got my mace always handy." She bent over and pulled out her purse to shake the little can of mace attached to her keys.

"Well, I will see this week. Bye Annie, behave!" She hugged the older woman and headed out the door.

She opened her phone again and began responding to Heather's messages.

Hey, sorry I haven't been very talkative lately, busy busy. I see you guys are having a blast though! I miss you and we need to have a wine night soon.

Not even a minute later, her phone buzzed back.

I was worried about you! I didn't want to bother you if you were busy with Cade. Also, Tommy has been all about staying disconnected so we could be together without the distractions. Anyways, I have some news when I get back. Love you!

Love you too! Cindy responded.

Curious what the news was, her mind began to wander. She looked at the time and knew she needed to get ready for her next self-defense course. Not to mention that she was supposed to be jogging tonight too. It had been years since she last jogged.

Back at her condo, she looked at her naked body in the mirror. Her new piercing shimmered in her navel and she poked at it to see if it was still sore. Her bed was still rumpled and unmade from that morning and she felt a stab of longing when she remembered how ready Cade was that morning. She ached to have him deep inside of her again.

Taking her phone, she snapped a nude shot of herself. Not liking the first angle, she took another and then another. Finally, she found one that she thought would make him crazy and sent it, nervous but surprisingly aroused by it too.

***

Cade looked at his phone and saw that Cindy had sent him another attachment. Painfully aware that he was not alone, he decided to wait until he could step in the back to open this one; best to not accidentally flash a customer with his girlfriend's underwear.

"I want you to put two smokin' guns on my right thigh and a candy skull below it," Cade's customer interrupted his fantasy.

CAde stared at the large area of pale skin and decided not to correct the woman. Most people called them sugar skulls, or the proper term was calavera. He didn't mind doing the art work, he just minded when someone called them by an incorrect name.

"Alright, it might sting right here, but I will make it look awesome, promise."

He smiled and his customer's face remained emotionless as he began the outline. Sometimes, when Cade was working, he would just be lost in thought. Ink blending with skin and his ability to recreate something on a human body. It had fascinated him when he had his first tattoo and he had always been a great artist. This was the first time in a while, that something had distracted him so much. He wanted to open that picture from Cindy. It was driving him mad. When his customer said she wanted a break before he continued, he smiled and jumped up. Her tattoo would start to burn and sting if he took too long so he ran to the back and closed the door behind him.

He looked at his phone and swiped to see what she had sent. Her naked body stretched out on the bed in a sexy pose, flashed back at him and he instantly felt himself grow rock hard. This woman was driving him insane.

Him: *You are making me a crazy man.*

Her: *Come over tonight after work. Unless you are too tired.*

Him: *See you soon.*

That was enough motivation to kick his butt into gear with the "smokin' guns and candy skull". When he had returned to the woman, her flesh was pink and raised and he got to work quickly. Sitting back, he looked at the beauty of his work before him. His customer smiled for the first time and thanked him for such a wonderful job. Not able to think about much of anything else, he made

sure that Alex and Cadence could close on their own. His
new hires were still waiting for the larger space. They
discovered how difficult it was to work with such little
room and now they would switch days with Alex or
Cadence. Sometimes working in the morning, afternoon,
or night. He even had the shop open later on the
weekends so they could log some time.

Leaving his business behind, he breathed in the
fresh cool air of the night and decided to head back to his
apartment before going over to Cindy's. He wanted to
take a shower and wash the smell of ink and sweat off.
From the time he left the shop, got to his apartment,
showered, and headed back to Cindy's he was certain only
thirty minutes had passed. She was looking down at him
from the balcony when he parked his bike in the usual
spot and walked towards her dark blue door.

She opened the door in a bright red, thin robe
and shut it behind them. Before he even had a chance to
say a word, she had walked over and crushed her mouth
against his. Her hands moved up his chest and back down
to hook under his shirt and pull it up and over his head.
She dropped the red robe to the ground exposing her
naked flesh underneath. Next she undid his pants and
pushed them down, as he quickly kicked them off. She
grabbed his throbbing hard cock from outside of his
underwear and squeezed. Moaning, he closed his eyes and
felt himself grow weak. Before he knew it, the passion
and desire completely consumed him and he picked her
up to take her up the stairs. She wrapped her legs around
him and he felt her hot wet center pushed against him.

Their mouths were locked when he sat her down
on the edge of her bed and started to lay her back. She
had something else in mind. She pushed him onto the
bed and climbed on top of him, centering herself just
above his throbbing head. Lowering herself down slowly,
he felt every inch of her surround him in a tight, warm

embrace. He moaned as she pushed down hard, grinding her hips into him and taking him in as far as she could. He cupped her breast in his hand and sucked on hard beaded flesh in front of him. Grabbing her hips, he slammed helped slam her down harder with each rise and fall of her perfect hips. Her moans vibrated from deep within and out as she squeezed him so tight and then gasped when the orgasm raked her body. Feeling her pulsing around him and going liquid, he pushed her down gently to on her back and plunged into her deep. His feet resting on the headboard giving him even more leverage to ram all the way back inside of her.

She cried out in pleasure and he felt her nails dig across his back and the heels of her feet push him in harder with each thrust. Her breasts moved with each rock of their hips and he sucked hard on the soft skin of her exposed neck. Feeling her grow closer to another climax, he groaned and slammed against her orgasm with his own. Filling her with his sex, they both panted from the ecstasy. She relaxed around his pulsing still hard member and he just rested on top of her, crushing her under his weight. She didn't seem to mind.

Finally, he pushed off of her and rolled onto his back. She moved to rest her head on his chest. Their hearts racing and pounding from their fevered sex.

"I love you babe."

"I love you." He kissed her deeply. They snuggled for a little bit but her soft skin against his aroused him and he moved to rest on top of her again.

Kissing her slowly, he moved up and down her body, relishing every inch of her. She moaned with each kiss and he stopped at her glistening mound, working her back into a frenzy. He felt her legs tremble as he kissed her softly there, teasing the light pink flesh. Cade kissed gently around her recent piercing and moved back up her midline. Coming back up to her breasts, he softly kissed and suckled their creamy flesh. When he knew she was ready for him again, he slowly entered her, thrusting with slow gentle movements. They made love, passionate and warm until their bodies were spent and he filled her once more with his orgasm. His legs were jelly this time and he soon drifted off into a peaceful sleep holding the woman he planned to spend forever with.

He could have made love to her all day if they had the time and the energy. When they both woke up, he was surprised that he wasn't rock hard with morning arousal. Their night of passion must have worn him out. He woke before she did and decided to try and have her breakfast made. Her kitchen was beautiful and pristine. He wondered if she ever cooked in it. Opening the door to her stainless steel fridge, he found that she had several premade meals packaged and labeled with dates and instructions.

Pushing the items to the side, he found the carton of eggs and a pouch of bacon and began frying and cooking. Smells of delicious breakfast permeated the condo and he wondered if she would wake soon from the smell alone. He looked at her coffee maker and after fiddling with it for a few minutes, he figured out how to start a pot brewing. It wasn't the bacon or the eggs that pulled her from her sleep, but the smell of the deliciously roasted beans that were freshly ground in the fancy machine. Perfectly pressurized water began running through, pushing smooth dark liquid into the glass pot below.

"That smells wonderful!" She complimented as she walked in wearing an oversized shirt and shorts.

Walking to a cabinet, she pulled out two large mouth coffee cups and filled them up with the steaming fresh brew.

"I am going to be busy with this upcoming event in the city," Cade started. "Cadence entered our shop into a contest and we won a booth at the event. I am going to wear a cape while I tattoo everyone, per Cadence's demands."

He finished his plate of food and started cleaning them up in the sink.

"Sounds like fun."

She brought him her empty plate and wrapped her arms around his waist, kissing him on the shoulder.

"So, I am supposed to have a round two at your parents?" Cade asked with a grimace.

He finished the dishes and left them to dry in a strainer on the kitchen. It didn't look like it had ever held a dish before.

"It looks like."

"Well," Cade continued with a sigh. "We need to go shopping for me something appropriate to wear."

"I haven't seen you dressed up since the wedding. You were so sexy in that tux."

"I will need your opinion for sure. I am a jeans and tee kind of guy if you haven't noticed."

"I think I can do that. They changed my schedule at the hospital, so I will have more time to do, exactly, what we did last night, any time." She placed her lips against his and wrapped herself around him.

"If you hadn't worn me out last night woman, I would bend you over this counter and make you scream."

Cade looked at his phone as it vibrated on the counter.

"Looks like Tommy is no longer disconnected."

"Ha, Heather was telling me about that yesterday. He made them ditch the phones for the most part."

"I don't blame him, I would too on our honeymoon."

Cade felt his heart leap into his throat. He hoped she didn't notice the slip.

"Hmm?" she purred.

She looked down into her empty cup of coffee and a noticeable shiver ran across her shoulders. He randomly craved a smoke and wondered if it would bother her if she knew he had a history with tobacco.

"Hey, I have never asked you this, but do you have a problem with cigarettes?"

"I am not a fan nor opposed. I sometimes really want one when I have had too much wine, but I can still remember the taste of my first one in college. It was bad! I threw up everywhere after, my head was spinning for the longest. Why?"

"Well, before I met you, I was a smoker. I haven't really had time to think or care about smokes with the past couple of eventful months."

"Oh. Well that's no problem, my father has a cigar any time he drinks a scotch. I prefer the smell of them to cigarettes, but that isn't a deal breaker. I definitely still love you."

"Good."

He watched her walk over to another cabinet and take out a pouch of pills. She took a glass from another cabinet and filled it with water from the sink, downing the pill. He wasn't going to pry, but he guessed his face was full was questions.

"Birth control," she stated plainly.

"Oh."

"You look so surprised."

"No, I just didn't even think to ask about that."

"I think that would have been an awkward conversation for sure. Um, excuse me, I know we just had sex and I came inside of you, but are you on birth control?"

He tickled her and smacked her on the butt as she snorted and ran away from him.

"I definitely don't sound like that," he complained.

"Oh, you should hear yourself."

Seeing her laugh and hearing her snort, he was enamored. An urge to ask her to marry him right then and there overwhelmed him, but he stuffed it down. He wanted to do this the right way, because he didn't plan to do it again. This woman drove him wild and made him laugh. She was smart and strong. She completed his puzzle and he needed to find the perfect ring to adorn her perfect hand with.

"I am going to head out and see what we need for the event next week." He kissed her on the cheek.

"Ok, I will see you tonight?" She looked hopeful.

"You bet."

His mind was made up and he made his way to the jewelry store. Once inside, who else would be there but her mother. Sighing, she turned and smiled at him, the smile never touching her eyes.

"Hello Cade," she fussed.

"Good afternoon Mrs. Watkins."

"What are you doing here?"

"Looking for something shiny for a beautiful lady."

"They are resetting the stone in my 1.5ct engagement ring and cleaning it while I am here," she explained without having been asked. "Cindy's grandmother passed it down to her father and he gave it to me. Cindy has always hated the thing. Says it is too 'clunky'. Anyways, she has always been a rather simple minded girl."

Her eyes moved up and down Cade and he tried really hard to conceal any annoyance.

"Well, she is a wonderful woman. She has a brilliant mind and a big heart."

"You are in love with her," Mrs. Watkins said plainly.

"Huh?"

"I can see it all over your face. Well, if I have to deal with you for the next half of my life, I get to help you pick out a ring for my daughter."

Cade wasn't sure to run or accept her help, but since it wasn't something he planned to just outright ask Cindy about, he let her mother help him.

They walked around the floor, staring into the glass at exquisite rings and bands. Colored gemstones jumped out at him and he saw the one he wanted to get her. Diamonds were placed equidistant around the thin band and in the center a perfect crystal blue aquamarine rested in its platinum mount.

"This is the one." Cade pointed at the ring and Cindy's mother scrutinized it.

"Well, it is rather small, are you sure you didn't like the tear drop set in rose gold?"

Her eyes had bulged at the sight of the ring and he knew she was only interested in it for herself.

"No, this is the one," Cade asserted.

Mrs. Watkins shrugged, disappointed but not arguing.

"What size should I go with Mrs. Watkins?"

"Cindy is a seven, I think."

Cade placed the order and went to set up the payments with the salesman.

"That will be two-thousand and thirty-five dollars."

Cade handed the man his card and waited as he ran it through their machine.

"Here you go sir," the salesman said, handing Cade back his card. "It is an exceptional ring for sure. We will have it ready in a few days."

"Thank you," Cade replied.

Mrs. Watkins was still hanging by the counter when Cade prepared to leave.

"You know, I didn't like you when we first met. I was so certain you were just some broke loser trying to mooch from my wealthy daughter."

"I honestly had no idea how wealthy you all were," Cade stumbled. "At least, not until visiting your beautiful home."

Mini castle, he thought.

"We will be having lunch at noon on Sunday. Then we like to go to the golf club. As long as you find yourself in fancier clothes, we would love for you to join us."

"If Cindy wants me there, I will be."

"Well, we will most likely see you then. She can't keep her eyes off of you as it is," her mother snickered and collected her things from the salesman. "I will see you Sunday Cade."

"Have a wonderful day Mrs. Watkins."

"That is a hard woman to please kid," the salesman added once Mrs. Watkins had gone.

Cade looked up at the salesman.

"Yea, my girlfriend's mom," Cade explained.

"Sounds like she will be your mother-in-law soon."

"Yea, hopefully."

"Good luck kid."

"Thank you."

Leaving the jewelry store, Cade suddenly felt a panic. He didn't think that Cindy and her mother were particularly close, but he hoped that her mother would not tell her he just spent the afternoon with her looking for a ring to propose with. Cade tried to push the worry from his mind and heading to the shop. Cadence greeted him with a serious face and a frown.

"We had a complaint today boss," she informed.

"What?"

"That new kid botched a job."

Cade sighed. "Oh no."

"Yea, so it turns out he is color blind. I am not sure what he gave you in his portfolio, but we have a seriously angry customer who expected her tattoo to be red and it is blue."

"Shit. Did we give her money back?"

"Of course."

"Good. I mean, that sucks, but good."

"Yea, except she wrote a formal complaint."

"Shit."

"Yea, it's online in plain view."

"Well, we could offer to bring her in and fix it, maybe?"

"Won't change the negative affects her comment placed on us."

"You're right," Cade conceded. "I guess we will just have to let the poor kid go and look at one of the other applicants."

"Yup."

"Ok, well thank you for keeping on top of it."

"That's what I do."

"Really, thank you Cadence."

"Um, you're welcome?"

"I am going to propose to Cindy and I am scared shitless," Cade blurted out, desperate to tell someone.

Cadence took a moment to process her boss' sudden statement.

"Well, don't be. The worst that can happen is she says no," she finally managed.

"That is exactly what I am afraid of," Cade said nervously as he ran his fingers through his hair.

"She will say yes."

"And how do you know?"

"Because she couldn't keep her eyes off of you and she talked about you while I pierced her navel. As a matter of fact, we talked about nothing else."

Cadence pretended to stick her finger down her throat, as if it made her sick to talk about him and Cindy.

"Enough about me, how is that little sea monkey in there?"

"Sea monkey?"

"Yea, I heard...oh never mind," Cade backpeddled.

Cadence cracked up at him.

"It is still early, but the doctor's said that everything looks pretty good for now."

"Good."

"Yup."

"Well, let's see what we are going to need for the event," Cade tried to steer the conversation back to business.

"I was thinking a table for starters."

"Ha."

With that, Cadence left and Cade got to work reading over the regulations for the event. That night he showed Cindy the plans for the event and nothing was mentioned about bumping into her mother at the store, or the purchase that he was waiting patiently for.

"Well, I think it sounds fun and if I wasn't working I would totally get dressed up and go," Cindy said, looking genuinely interested.

"When is your birthday?" Cade asked suddenly.

"Oh, ummm. June third, you?"

"October twentieth... I never celebrate my birthday though."

"Well, we'll have to change that. So what else did you do today?"

He felt his heart skip.

"Not a lot of anything exciting, you?"

"Oh, I enjoyed a pint of ice cream," Cindy started and Cade was relieved. "Which I am sure Maggie will not let me hear the end of. Hey, I wanted to show you the move she taught me yesterday, but we were busy in the bed last night and I forgot."

Memories of the night before tugged at his mind.

"Ok, let's see it," he agreed.

"Ok, we need to stand up. Um, let's move to the rug."

He followed her and she told him to pretend he was attacking her. She wrapped her leg around his own and quickly maneuvered him to the ground. She didn't use a lot of force, and he knew he move so he allowed her to pull him into it.

"Very good," he complimented.

She was holding him down, just slightly bending his arm back.

"It took me several tries, but I finally landed it. I was so excited."

"I am glad."

"Then she had me jog half a mile. I was so tired, but it felt so good at the same time."

"I could start jogging with you, if you wanted."

"That could be fun, but I am slow," She confessed.

She tucked her hair behind her ear and he sighed. He needed a creative way to propose to her.

14

Cade's mind was busy with ways to propose to the woman of his dreams as he sat at the table handing out fliers and waiting for the time they could begin tattooing. Several people came in wearing recognizable superhero costumes, and others were not so recognizable. Either way, it was a huge outpouring of support from the community and many avid readers and lovers of comic books flooded through the doors of the event.

"What is this?" A young man poked at the wheel behind Cade, bringing him out of his stupor.

"You can spin it if you want," Cade explained. "You will either win a tattoo, piercing, or a tattoo design of my choice. Would you like to give it a go?"

The young man nodded and spun the wheel. It landed on the space that allowed Cade to design the tattoo.

"Ok," Cade started. "For this you need to pick three words that best describe you."

He saw the young man think about it for a second.

"Spontaneous, geek, and outer space."

Cade's mind surged with ideas, and he began on the drawing before he would tattoo. He may have made this a fun little game, but he was also going to give the kid the best. When he was done, he showed his sketch to the young man and he nodded.

"I would love that as a tattoo!" The young man exclaimed. "Preferably on my forearm."

Cade nodded and got to work.

Through the day they ended up with only three that landed on that space and Cade enjoyed all three, but the first one was the most memorable. As the day wound down Cade and Cadence finished up with the customers. Cadence collected their things and took her time visiting the other booths before closing. Cade simply sat and passively watched the dwindling crowd, his mind focused on figuring out how to propose.

***

Cade and Cindy spent most of their free time in each other's company as the days turned into weeks and before she realized, it had been more than a month since she last slept in her bed a full night without Cade. Her cast had been removed and all that was left was a soreness as her bones readjusted to life outside the cast. Tommy and Heather had gotten back from their adventure honeymoon, and insisted on catching up with Cade and Cindy.

"So what's new man?" Tommy asked once he and Cade were finally together again.

"Well, Cadence is expecting a baby and engaged to Alex. I final found the location I want to move my business to, and I am planning to propose to Cindy as soon as I can figure out the perfect way to do it."

"Whoa. I missed a lot while out adventuring," Tommy chuckled. "Cadence and Alex? Really?"

Cade laughed and took a sip of his beer.

"Yea, they have been together for a while I am sure, but they recently stopped hiding it from me."

"Well good for them. Hey, that is great about you and Cindy. I am shocked because you two seem very different, but together you look really happy."

"She is something."

"So, Heather and I have some news of our own," Tommy said with a sly grin. "Looks like Cadence and Alex won't be the only new parents."

Cade sat back and stared at his best friend.

"Look at you Tommy. You are a big news anchorman, married to the love of your life, and you are going to be a dad. That's awesome. I am buying tonight, don't you dare try."

Cade looked over to where Heather and Cindy stood by the pool table. They were setting the table up for a game and he imagined Cindy's round belly full of child, his child. The thoughts gave him goose bumps.

"You could do one of those theater announcements," Tommy suggested. "Take her to a movie and at the end of the credits have the screen pop up with 'will you marry me'."

"I don't know. I want it to be special, personal."

Tommy shook his head. "Well, when the time comes you will know. Trust me. Just like you knew she was the one, you will know when you should ask."

"I hope so."

"Let's go join the girls," Tommy motioned with his head. "Looks like Heather finally told Cindy."

When Cade glanced back at the girls, Cindy was hugging Heather and placing her hand on her tummy.

A pang of jealousy landed in Cindy's own belly as she touched her best friends. She wondered about the life that was growing deep in there. Would it be a boy or a girl? Her own empty womb ached to have a baby. She had never worried about her "internal clock", but now that most of her friends were married with their own families, it seemed like she was a ticking time bomb. Cade and Tommy joined them at the pool table, and Tommy whispered something in Heather's ear, causing her to blush and smile. They were radiating with joy.

Cade wrapped his arms around Cindy and she felt safe; jealousy evaporating with his touch.

"I can't believe they are going to have a baby," Cindy cooed to Cade.

"I know," he whispered back.

She felt his lips brush across her neck and she caught her breath. Excitement pulsed below as he held his hands around her waist. Warmth radiating from those hands and she longed to carry his child.

When they were done playing a few rounds of pool, she convinced him to take her back to her condo. Cade had been acting funny that week and Cindy wondered what was going on with him.

"You've been quiet," she prodded.

Cade was sitting at her table working on a drawing for his scheduled custom tattoos. His art was beautiful. She looked at his work and admired it as she had that first blissful night at his apartment.

"I have had a lot on my mind lately," he tried to deflect.

"Anything you want to talk about?"

He set his pen down and stared at her. The intensity of those green eyes on her, made her uneasy. Slowly, he got up from his spot and walked towards her. Stopping in front of her, he took her chin in his hand and pointed it up at him. He placed his mouth on hers and kissed her sweetly; then rested his forehead on hers as he held her, rocking side to side.

"Cade?"

"I wanted to make this perfect," he admitted. "But I think we are already as perfect as we can get. I know that it isn't always going to be easy. I know that you won't always like me. You won't always be happy with the things that I want to do. Our opinions are different, because we are different, but I am so madly in love with you just the same."

He took out the ring that had been resting in his pocket for days.

"Cindy, I could get down on one knee and ask you to marry me. I could shout it from the rooftops, or even hire a choreographed group to start singing and dancing. The truth is, I just want to hold you and keep you safe. I want to be the one that you share your long day at the hospital with and I want to wake up beside you every morning for the rest of my life. This ring reminded me of those beautiful crystal blue eyes that cared for me when I had been stabbed in an alley and left to die. I love you and will always love you, if you will let me."

He held the ring out to her and Cindy just stared at it. His hand held the most beautiful ring she had ever seen. She reached out to lightly touch it and saw that his hands were trembling.

"Yes. Of course," she whispered, barely able to speak.

She took his face in her hands and placed a kiss on his lips; tears filling her eyes from his sweet proposal. He carried her to the couch and made love to her.

15

Cindy sat at her nurse's station the next day, unable to keep her eyes off the ring adorning her finger. Her mind was awash in the possibilities the future weeks were to bring.

"What is that beautiful little treasure on your finger?" Annie looked over her gold rimmed glasses.

"Cade proposed."

She was so full of joy and excitement, it was spilling from her.

"Well, congratulations Cindy. That is wonderful news! Too bad Dr. Twat isn't here anymore. This would send him off the deep end."

Todd had successfully opened up his practice. Cindy's mother always keeping tabs on the young doctor, had informed her he was seeing one of his nurses there. She felt both sorry for the girl he was stringing along and happy that she wouldn't be on his radar anymore.

"Yea, I am glad I do not have to deal with that drama," Cindy chuckled.

"Time to start plannin' that weddin'," Annie declared. Cindy looked at her incredulously. "What?" Annie defended herself. "It's never too early to weddin' plan!"

Cindy could already see the wheels turning and knew that if she didn't escape now, Annie would have her trying on wedding dresses down the street while they were supposed to be working. Luckily a call light warned her that she was needed and she used it to get away.

A blur of people rushed through the emergency room doors as the EMT's handed their patient off to the hospital staff. Cindy rushed to join them and an alarm went off in her chest when a familiar mop of red was wheeled in on a gurney.

"We pulled a middle-aged Jane Doe from a wreck. We think she is pregnant, her pulse is thread," the EMT called out as everyone rushed down the hall.

They were busy working on her as Cindy grew closer and was able to get a better look. Her heart sank when Cindy saw her best friend was stretched out on the gurney. Her face was bruised and broken.

"The red-head, was she the driver?" Cindy inquired of the EMT following closely behind.

"Uh, no," he responded. "No she wasn't the driver, but the driver was DOA so we moved to rescue her. Their car was flipped on top of itself and crushed. She will be lucky if she survives."

Cindy turned away from the kid, he had no idea that throwing out that simple abbreviation had just shattered her world. DOA. Dead on arrival. Sensitivity is taught to the medical professionals, but he most likely had no idea he just delivered earth shattering news to basically family in a nonchalant way. Cindy excused herself for a moment and ducked into a nearby bathroom. She held her stomach and heaved; nausea and terror ripping her insides as she just hoped that somehow it wasn't Tommy driving. She knew it was though. Of course it was Tommy driving.

They brought his lifeless body in a bag after they had delivered those that needed medical immediate medical care. Cindy was not allowed to work on Heather. She had walked into the room, blurry eyed and flushed. As soon as they knew it was her best friend, they made her take a seat in the lobby.

"Call their next of kin Cindy. Call someone for you. We will keep you posted on her status as we know more." They said the same things that Cindy said to her patients, every single day.

Numbness set in and she wanted to call Cade, but was terrified of sharing such crushing news with him. Opening up their last text message, she thought she could at least handle that over talking.

Her: *Can you get away to come visit at the hospital?*

Him: *Sure. I just have to wrap up things with this half sleeve and I will be on my way.*

She wondered how she would tell him that his best friend and only thing close to family was dead, while his pregnant wife fought for her life in one of these rooms. Next she called Mr. and Mrs. Lane and then Heather's parents. Trying to stay as calm as possible, she just explained to them that there had been an accident and that it was best if they came on to the hospital. Thirty minutes later, the two sets of parents were standing in the same lobby with Cindy when Cade walked in.

He took one look at her red puffy eyes and saw Tommy's parents and Heather's. She could see the anguish and fear that flashed into those deep greens.

"Cindy, what, what's going on?" Cade asked franticly.

At that moment two doctors walked out and took the sets of parents in different rooms. Cindy sat back down and patted the seat next to her. Thankful she didn't have to tell Tommy's parent's but her heart was weighed with grief as she prepared herself to tell Cade.

"Cade, there was an accident. Tommy…Tommy passed away. They have Heather in the back now, but it doesn't look good. I think they were talking about possibly delivering the baby. She is twenty-eight weeks, so it is possible that the baby will survive. It is also possible that Heather will not."

A sob escaped her lips and she fought back the tears that threatened to overflow again. Cade sat there motionless. Tommy and Heather's parents each stepped out of the rooms, faces full of sadness and sorrow as they held each other for comfort.

"Cindy sweetie," Heather's mom managed. "Have... have they said anything else about the baby?"

"No ma'am, just what they told you," Cindy responded.

"Ok."

Heather's mom was holding Tommy's mother in her arms. She patted her, consoling her for the loss of her son and trying to provide her any bit of strength she could as she fretted for her own child. Tommy's and Heather's dads sat solemn, two stoic and silent figures who were holding themselves together as their wives broke down in tears.

Hours passed, and Cade still sat in silence. His face was hard, but Cindy could see the pain in those eyes. She just held his hand and rubbed his arm as she watched the clock tick by. Finally, a doctor came out to talk to them.

"We were able to deliver the baby, and she is so strong. We are expecting a full recovery for her. As for Heather, we cannot say until some of the swelling on her brain goes down. I am so sorry, she may wake up or she may never wake up. We have done everything that we can for her now and we will just keep monitoring her and the swelling."

Heather's mother trembled and a soft wail poured out from her. Tommy's mother was now the one to hold her as she cried. Cindy's heart hurt at the sound of a broken mother. She had heard it more than once, but never from someone she had spent years getting know and love. Her own heart ached with pain and for the first time since he heard about his best friend's sudden death, Cade wrapped his arm around Cindy and pulled her in close.

They held a funeral for Tommy days after his passing. It had to be closed casket due to the damage to his face in the wreckage. Heather's condition did not seem to improve and they were afraid they may have to take her off life support in the next couple of weeks. At this point, they were afraid that she would be a vegetable if she ever did wake. Cade looked down at the mahogany casket that held his friend. It seemed so small. Just a few months ago, they had played pool and Cade found out they were expecting a baby.

How can he be dead?

Tommy's baby was fighting in the neonatal intensive care unit. Cade would go and visit the little beauty and he was even able to let her wrap her tiny hand around his finger. She was so small that she could have fit in his hand. So many wires and ports were connected to her small body. He was almost thankful that Tommy and Heather were not there to see her like that. She didn't even have a name. They had talked about a few names but never settled on one. For now, baby Lane, was all that her read on her name plate.

Cade watched as they lowered Tommy's coffin into the ground and poured the dirt over the top. Cindy was there, holding a sobbing Mrs. Lane. Cade sighed and looked to the sky above. He spoke, unsure if he was trying to speak to Tommy or himself.

"I can't believe you're gone man. I won't see your smug face on the news anymore. That little girl of yours is a fighter, you would be so proud. I am not sure what happens when we die or where we go, but I know that if Heather has to join you soon, you will be happy and your little girl will be cared for. Don't you worry. I will make sure she gets to school on time and that little boys leave her alone; even if I have to use a baseball bat to run them off. I am going to drink one for you tonight. Tonight is on me, so don't you dare try anything."

His eyes filled with tears and he felt their cool stream slide down his cheek. It was the first time he allowed himself to cry since learning of Tommy's death.

Cade was the last to leave the cemetery, joining Cindy who was waiting in the car. She never rushed him, or asked any questions. She placed a warm hand on his leg and gave him a comforting squeeze as they left a fresh unmarked grave. A week later, they had to say goodbye to Heather. They buried her beside Tommy and when their headstones came in they both read: *Gone too soon but not forgotten, loving mother and father to baby Cynthia Lane.*

16

Cade took a few weeks off from work. He cancelled and rescheduled his appointments. Their new location was larger and much more open. They had even picked up a few more artists. Cade's accountant had helped him crunch the numbers, and it wasn't as daunting as it had once seemed. He was making enough from the busy influx of customers to offset the cost of their move. Many of their regulars thought they would be upset with the change, but found they liked the new parlor even more than the old.

Cade was hunched over a young man, working on a tiger pouncing from his bicep when the young man spoke up.

"I was so scared this place was going to be shitty, but this is awesome dude!"

He had been adding ink to this kid for years and he knew how outspoken Charlie could be.

"Glad it isn't shitty," Cade joked as he continued to add detail to the tiger's fur.

"Oh yea, man, we are super stoked about it. I mean, you have so much space now and you also are in a more convenient location. I think you are going to see some pretty heavy traffic."

Charlie's prediction was accurate and their business was booming. Finishing up the final touches, he sat back and stared at his work. What once brought him joy, was now just another job to him. He wasn't as pleased with the tiger as he wanted to be, but the kid was happy   about   it.

"That looks awesome!"

Cade was glad that his customer was happy and he collected his payment. His next customer was a middle-aged woman who had emailed him a picture of her deceased grandbaby days before. His heart broke for her and he made sure he had time for her special portrait. The baby's cheeks were perfectly round and healthy in the picture. Two little grey eyes peeped out and he wondered what happened to the little guy.

"Hanna?" Cade called from the front desk.

She stood up and moved into the back of the parlor with him. She set her things down and took a seat in chair.

"Where do you want baby Everett?" He was trying to be as kind and personal as possible, letting her know he took this request very seriously, and that he paid attention to her email.

"My right bicep," her voice was just a whisper, but he began the outline and placed the image of the sweet baby on her arm.

He added a little shading and rosy cheeks to bring the baby to life. The image now forever resting in peace on her arm.

"Do you mind if I may ask," Cade stumbled. "What happened?"

"Oh… well he was just sleeping in his crib. Happy, healthy little baby. My daughter was breastfeeding him and he was growing just fine, but then one night she went to check on him and he wasn't breathing. They called 911, but by the time they arrived, he was gone."

"I am so sorry for your loss Hanna." He gripped her hand in his and saw the tears in the bottom of her eyes.

"Thank you. It's beautiful."

They moved to the front of the shop and she came to the counter to pay.

"This one is one me," he told her, tears well up in his own eyes.

She thanked him and he closed out her session. Before he could leave and call the next customer she pulled him into a hug.

"Whatever pain you feel now child, it will pass. Pain is fleeting," she assured him.

She left him there standing shocked by those words. Those very same words that Spencer had said almost a year ago, sending a chill down his spine.

* * *

Wedding planning had stopped for a brief period as everyone was suspended in mourning. Even Cindy's parents didn't push the date or plans. However, the days were ticking by and before she even knew it, her wedding was scheduled for the next weekend.

"Cindy, you have your last dress fitting tomorrow dear," her mother called out from her kitchen.

"Okay."

Cindy had lost a couple inches after Tommy and Heather's death; stress and shock ruining any chance of an appetite. She also spent most of her time visiting baby Cynthia, who was growing so strong, and Cindy hoped that she would be able to go home soon. Tommy's parents were the first to volunteer to take care of the little one. Cindy felt a tug at her heart every time she held Cynthia. She wanted to take her home, but they would follow the wishes in the wills of their beloved friends.

In just a few days, she would be Mrs. Cade Winters. Her heart was excited, but she still grieved for the maid of honor that wouldn't stand by her side and the best man that wouldn't have Cade's back. They chose a small venue, which had upset her mother, but she did a good job of keeping her mouth shut. Since Cade had no living relatives he knew of, Cindy didn't want to invite a huge number of guests either. He had told her to have the wedding of her dreams, he was happy as long as he was standing next to her at the end of it all.

"Let's go. I just remembered we still need to find you shoes." Her mother snapped her fingers, as if that would make Cindy move any faster.

A few hours and several bags later, she was certain they had everything for this wedding. She was fitted for her gown one last time, and then the next day was the big day.

Everything that could go wrong did. Her hair was being unruly and they were running late bringing the cake to the venue. When she slipped into the shoes, which her mother had insisted they buy, blisters formed on her heels and toes before she had walked five feet. Fearing the worst on what was supposed to be her special day, she sat down in a chair and cupped her hands around her face. Just then a knock sounded on the door and Cadence walked in.

"Hey beautiful, we need you to get out here so we can get this shindig started. Also, we're hungry."

Cadence's stomach was large and round. She looked like she had swallowed a watermelon. It looked good on her petite form and she still wore her punk and gothic style clothes, she just purchased several sizes too large.

"I feel like some celestial being is cursing me and if I go out there," Cindy sobbed. "I am going to fall and break my collarbone or something equally ominous."

"Oh honey, that is just the jitter bugs. Everyone feels that way before they get hitched. Trust me. Well, I have never had them, but I have heard of them anyways."

Cindy shook her head and looked to the plump goth standing at her door. "Look at you, you are glowing. Aren't you due this week?"

"I was due last week," Cadence laughed through a samile.

The pair started laughing so hard that before she even knew what was happening, a gush of liquid poured from between Cadence's legs.

"I... I think my water just broke," Cadence squeaked out before letting out a moan and bent back in pain.

Labor pains came on quickly and Cindy stuck her head out and called for help. Cade ran in at the sound of her alarmed voice. He took one look at Cadence who was now sitting in a chair breathing heavy with her hands on her belly. Her lap was wet and he quickly ran out to grab Alex. Alex flew into the room and with the help of Cindy, they walked Cadence to their car and climbed in. Cade ran to his decorated bike and jumped on, ribbons and cans with a just married sign stuck to the back followed close behind the speeding car with blinking hazards.

Cindy was sitting in the back of Alex's care holding Cadence's hand as she moaned and sucked in breath, her tight belly bulging under the fabric of her dress. They rushed through the automatic doors of the hospital and they checked her on quickly.

"Baby is already crowning, let's get her on a bed and rush her to L&D," the nurse called out.

Cindy never let go of Cadence's hand and Alex held the other as they rushed beside her to the delivery wing. It didn't take long before their baby boy entered this world. Cadence, exhausted but only concerned with one thing turned to Cindy who still held her hand.

"Is he ok?" Cadence asked, still trembling from exhaustion as they worked to deliver her afterbirth.

Finally letting go of Cindy's hand she looked over to the baby warmer where the nurses worked quickly to clean and suction the little perfectly pink and plump baby. Worried because he hadn't cried yet, Cindy moved closer as hands frantically worked to clear his airway. Not even a second later, the first little cries squealed from their newborn baby and Cindy sighed with relief.

"He is perfect," Cindy assured.

"May I hold him?" Cadance asked, reaching towards the nurse cleaning up their wailing newborn.

"Of course, you may."

They placed her new bundle in her arms, and Cadence's face erupted with joy. Alex was by her side, cradling her head and cooing at their tiny little human.

Cindy excused herself to go find Cade in the lobby. She found him wringing his hands, knuckles white as he was clearly in a state of distress. They had too much happen lately and he was worried yet another things was going to go wrong. Walking towards her future husband, Cindy sat down beside him and placed her small hands on his.

"The baby is perfect. Alex and Cadence are perfect. We are all just perfect."

He turned those green eyes on her and his eyes moved up and down the length of her body.

"You look amazing," he acknowledged his bride to be, still in her wedding dress.

All of the worry that was there before was replaced with admiration.

"Thank you."

She looked down at her dress. It was made out of a soft material that was fitted to accent her thin waist and hour glass shape. From the hips down, it fell naturally down the length of her body. Lace rimmed the bottom of her gown and rested softly on her shoulders. Small pearls were stitched into the front of the gown in an intricate design, and her hair was pulled half way up, while the rest was curled. Her makeup was light and natural.

"You look pretty handsome yourself," she returned and smiled at him.

She wrapped her arm around his, resting her head on his shoulder. They had only been sitting that way a moment, when Alex came from around the corner.

"Cadence asked, well told me, to come tell you guys to go. Go get married. We are fine here and you can come back after if you want." He smiled at the pair and Cade stood to hug him.

"Congratulations man!" Cade patted Alex on the back.

"Thanks and you too."

Next, Cindy stepped up to hug him.

"He is beautiful Alex," she said in their embrace.

Cindy moved back to Cade. He wore a button down white shirt with grey slacks. He looked comfortable and laid back. She knew he held a lot of tension inside from the stress they had both endured.

"Do you think we can go visit Cynthia?" Cade had stopped and looked at the elevator.

"Yea, let's go," Cindy agreed.

Once upstairs, they found Tommy's mom rocking baby Cynthia.

"Hey," Cade greeted her as he rested a hand on her shoulder and peered down at the sleeping sweet baby in Mrs. Lane's arms.

"Hey, why aren't you two at your wedding?"

While she had grieved for the loss of her son, she had filled her sorrow with joy and love for little Cynthia. Now, she glared at Cade and if she hadn't been holding the baby she would have probably been poking him in the chest with one hand on her hip.

"Cadence went into labor before the wedding even started," Cade explained.

"Oh dear, is she still in labor?"

"No, she delivered quickly. Everyone is ok and downstairs resting."

"Oh good. At least she didn't labor for hours and hours. When I was in labor with Tommy, it took almost three days to get him out. They even used this gas on me to make me sleepy and ease my pain. He was always so stubborn."

Her eyes glistened from the tears that threatened to form.

"Well, it looks like little Ms. Cynthia took some of his stubbornness. She is a fighter."

Cade stuck his finger in her little hand and she gripped on tight. Seeing him with a baby, Cindy felt her chest tighten.

"Would you like to hold her?" Mrs. Lane asked, offering the baby to Cade.

"Uh, sure, is that ok?"

Mrs. Lane chuckled and stood up. He looked nervous but once Mrs. Lane placed Cynthia in his arms, his shoulders relaxed and he looked so natural with that baby in his arms.

"You know that you two are the godparents?"

Cindy and Cade both jerked their heads at Mrs. Lane.

"What?" They asked in unison.

"Tommy and Heather had their suspicions about you two for some time. They added you guys to their will, as the godparents of their unborn children. They figured that one way or another, they would bring you two together. At first, Tommy was a little skeptical, but after you two started dating he and Heather knew you guys were perfect for each other. I think you two had better go finish those wedding vows."

She reached back over to collect Cynthia and Cade seemed almost hesitant to give her up. Cindy hugged Mrs. Lane and kissed Cynthia's sweet head, inhaling her scent. Taking Cade by the arm, they left the hospital and made their way back to their wedding.

Thankfully, the guests had just been eating in the dining hall when they arrived and the pastor was still available to finish the ceremony. What had started out ominous turned into a beautiful and happy wedding.

They had written their own vows for the event and Cade's voice and hands trembled as he read his own words aloud.

"Cindy, it has been a long and interesting year. When I first saw you standing there in that purple number, my heart stopped and you were all I could see. I still remember holding you for the first time as we danced at our dear friend's wedding and I knew I could hold you for the rest of my life. I promise to always love you, and to protect you, even if you are now strong enough to protect yourself. My past was rocky, but my future is bright, with you by my side as my loving, and beautiful wife."

He folded the paper back up and placed it in his pant pocket and slipped a shimmering band on her ring finger. She had memorized her lines, but still unfolded her paper. Looking him straight in those blue eyes, she began.

"Cade, you are my balance beam. I have never felt more alive or free to be myself than when I am with you. You're the most talented, adventurous, and handsome man I have ever known. Your kindhearted soul draws me in and holds me close. I promise to love you forever, to treat you with kindness, and hold you up when you are down. We have overcome so much together and I hope to overcome so much more by your side."

She placed his simple white gold band on his ring finger and they held hands, eyes locked on one another. Before the pastor could finish his words, Cade had pulled her close and kissed her softly. Everyone else in the room disappeared and it was just the two of them, standing there, enveloped in one another. He pulled back and smiled, then kissed her one more time. They turned to their laughing guests and walked out and to the dining hall. Everyone lined up to visit them and Cindy saw an older man walk up to Cade and place his hand on Cades shoulder.

"Son, you done good." He leaned in and hugged Cade.

"Thanks Hank," Cade smiled. "And thank you for coming."

Hank, leaned in and pointed his finger at Cindy.

"I told him to go get his girl and he did just that!" He smiled and nodded, clearly satisfied with himself.

"Yes, you did Hank. Thank you again. You have always been my life saver."

"Well, you better be turning to the Mrs. now kid, I am getting too old," he huffed and with that made his way to help himself to more food.

Next Annie stepped up and took Cade's hand in hers, yanking him down to eye level.

"Remember what I told you boy? About my special concoction?"

Cindy rolled her eyes, but saw Cade nod, a smile twitching around the corners of his mouth. She saw slight stubble around his mouth and chin and smiled. Maybe after things settled down, she could convince him to grow his beard back out.

"Well, it still stands that if you ever hurt this sweet young lady, I will bring down somethin' truly sinister on ya'."

"Yes ma'am." He entertained the old woman and Cindy just laughed.

"Now, sug', who is that fine man that was just talkin' to you two?" Annie asked, looking straight at Hank.

"Who, Hank?" Cade answered, and Annie's eyes darted back to him.

"I like the sound of that, Hank."

She rolled the name around as if she was trying it out and made her way to stand behind Hank. They watched as she pretended to bump into him as she reached to grab a new plate. At first he seemed a little confused and flustered, but after a few minutes and some obvious flirting they were laughing and clearly enjoying each other.

"Isn't that something?" Cindy asked and looked at Cade, who she found was staring at her.

"Yes. Now, may I have this dance, Mrs. Winters?"

She felt her heart pick up in pace. She was married. Her. She was really married, and to Cade.

"Always."

They moved to the middle of the dance floor and he wrapped his arms around her as they swayed to the music. As she rested her head against him, her mind drifted to the events that had led to this moment. She had not thought about Spencer in some time, too busy with funerals and work. Thoughts of that day in captivity would always be with her, but the pain and trauma had faded. Her heart still ached for Heather and her baby who would never know her mother, a raw ache in her chest and sadness for the loss of her best friend. At the same time, joy warred with the grief as she thought about Alex and Cadence and their new bundle of joy. On top of it all, she was dancing with her husband.

"Cade?"

"Yes my love."

"We have never talked about this before, and now may not be the best time...but, well," Cindy paused as they sway for a few moments. "Never mind."

"What is it? You can ask me anything." His green eyes stared into her own blue's.

"Well, I was wondering if you wanted children?"

She felt his grip tighten around her and he was silent for a moment.

"I do want children. I am scared to death of the parent I will be, but yes, I want children, with you. As a matter of fact, I would love to get started right away."

She could see the desire in his half-closed eyes and felt him growing hard against her. Despite how many times she had been with Cade, his lust for her and her own arousal at just his touch surprised her.

She was breathtaking, even though he had already seen her in her dress, when Cindy had walked down the aisle towards him, Cade stopped breathing for a moment. She was full of confidence, which when he had first seen her in that purple dress at Tommy's wedding, she seemed the complete opposite. Her confidence made her radiate warmth and joy and he was happily drowning in it. Now he held her in his arms on the dance floor, his mind busy with the idea of children. He had always wanted children, but had never found someone to share his life or heart with until her. Imagining her belly round with his child excited him and now that he had admitted to wanting to start right away, it was all he could do to not skip the rest of this wedding ritual and get to work practicing with her.

Seeing the lust form in her eyes, he decided he would tease her the rest of the night until they tumbled in the sheets as husband and wife. He wanted to see what she would do if he teased her for an extended time. Bending down, he lightly kissed her neck and then moved back to her.

"I can't wait to get you naked tonight and have my way with you," he whispered beside her ear.

He heard her suck air between those perfect pink lips and kissed her ear. She pressed into him, her hips ever so discreetly rubbing against him.

This is going to be fun.

When the song stopped, he pulled back and headed for food, leaving her dazed. They set down to eat, he placed his hand on her thigh and slowly inched up between her legs. Her dress was too thick for him to tease her as much as he wanted, but he could tell that just touching her was driving her crazy. She playfully slapped at his hand away and he smiled.

His last attempt to make Cindy crazy was when he went searching for her garter. He moved his hand up the length of her leg and feeling the lacey garter, moved passed it just a little higher. His fingers grazed her and she slightly squeezed her thighs together, warning him he would be in big trouble if he didn't get that garter and go. Her eyes were narrowed at him, but lust raged behind them.

"You just wait Mr. Winters."

"Oh, I can't."

He smiled wide and she blushed. Not wanting to prolong their evening, they rushed the rest of the usual activities and headed to the decorated bike. A can had been lost on the way to the hospital, and the just married sign was now crooked, but Cindy was still excited to hop on and hug her husband.

"Take me home, now," she whispered in his ear, before he started the loud engine and they waved goodbye to their family and friends.

They had decided to stay in her condo, which was a hard decision. They loved his apartment in the city, but the condo had space for them to grow in that the apartment did not. When they parked the bike, Cade scooped Cindy up and carried her through the front door of their home. They didn't made it up the stairs.

He carefully pulled her gown from her body and undressed himself. Cade wanted to be deep inside of her, but teasing her had proven to be so fun earlier that he wanted to continue what he started. He kissed and caressed her all over, toying with the sensitive spots that are meant to drive a woman wild until he felt her body quake.

"Cade, I need you inside me now!"

"No. Not yet."

He was enjoying this too much. Her body squirmed and trembled and he brought her to the edge over and over.

"Please," she begged, her voice was strained and frantic with desire.

When he brought her to the edge for the last time, he slammed deep inside of her and relished the waves of orgasm that swept through her and over him. That night, he made love to her until she physically couldn't go anymore.

He kissed her and pulled her exhausted body against his own. He wouldn't let her know just how spent he was. When they woke the next morning, their legs were intertwined and he was spooning her naked body. He stretched and felt the muscles in his legs and core scream from the excessive use that night. Slowly, trying not to wake her, he slipped his arm out from under her and moved to the kitchen for coffee. Walking on shaking legs, he felt off balanced. Cindy woke up to the smell of coffee and he smiled. She was clearly on auto pilot as he watched her pull her medicine pouch from the cabinet and fill a glass with water. Before she got the pill to her mouth, she stopped and looked at Cade. Realizing that she wasn't going to take those anymore, she smiled and threw the pill in the trash.

"I guess I won't be needing those anymore," she purred to her lover.

"Nope."

17

As their first week of post-marital bliss came to a close, Cade stretched and prepared to head into the shop.

"Do you have to go to work today?" She pouted her lip and batted those beautiful eyes at him.

"Sadly, yes. I need to swing by the shop and see how things have been going while I have been away."

"Well, just hurry back home so we can have a repeat of last night."

With that, she turned and slowly walked away with her cup of coffee. Before disappearing around the corner, he saw her pull off her robe and look back at him. It was the sexiest thing he had ever seen. He forced himself to leave and made his way downtown to his business.

Cade walked into the front doors and found his new hires busy working on customer's tattoos and piercings. Two were adding the finishing touches to their customer's tattoos and another one was preparing to pierce a lip. He missed Alex and Cadence and wondered what they were up to.

Cade: *Hey Cadence, how have you been? How is the baby?*

Cadence: *Hey boss, we are great. Look behind you.*

Cadence and Alex approached him with a car seat in tow. He saw how big their baby had gotten in such a short time and was shocked at the sight of all that hair.

"We named him Oliver," Cadence beamed.

"Hi Oliver," Cade said with a smile.

He reached down and touched the soft black hair on the baby's head. Oliver stretched and yawned, but didn't wake.

"Is there anything we can do today?" Alex inquired.

"You came to work, with your baby?" Cade asked, one eyebrow raised and Cadence just stared at him.

"Yea. He just sleeps and when he cries I just stick a boob I his mouth," Cadence laughed. "It's ok. He'll be fine."

She seemed so comfortable as a new mom. Cade just laughed and shrugged.

"Look at the schedule if you want."

Since they moved to the bigger building, they had also upgraded to a new scheduling system. They still kept ledgers in case their systems were down, but preferred to use the computer scheduling program.

"Sweet. There are tons of piercing requests for today. I got this."

She began typing away, confirming appointment times. Alex leaned against the counter, never one for many words.

"So, how is married life?" Alex inquired.

"Pretty awesome, I mean it has only been a week."

He grinned and they shared a look.

"Are you going to be adding one of these to your family soon?" Alex pointed at his chubby little sleeping baby.

"We shall see."

"Well good luck. So far, Ollie man has been awesome. He sleeps through the night most nights and is happy for the most part. He craps a lot and spits up on everything, but he is pretty chill."

***

Cade and Cindy had tried for a few months to get pregnant with no luck. Reluctantly, Cindy went to see the doctor. They ran labs on her and checked her out, but didn't find anything wrong with her. As they sat in the examination room, Cade watched the doctor go over various options for conceiving.

"You have to be trying for a year or more before we begin injections or pills to increase fertility. Since you have only been trying for a few months and Cindy, you have been on the pill for years, it is possible it will take some time to clear your system so you can become pregnant."

She just nodded her head.

"What about me?" Cade asked the doctor as the doctor turned to leave the room.

"Hmm?"

"Don't I need to be tested? It could be me shooting blanks," Cade sighed.

"We can definitely test your count, but I really think we need to first see what the results of Cindy's examination are, and give her time to completely remove the birth control from her system."

"Ok."

Leaving the doctor's office, they were still hopeful that they would successfully conceive. Cade's phone buzzed in his pocket and Mrs. Lane's number flashed on the screen.

"Hey Cade, how are you doing?" She asked with a baby crying in the background.

"Doing well and you?"

"We are fine. Sleep deprived, but fine."

"Can I help you with anything Mrs. Lane?"

"Well, we were hoping to discuss some things with you and Cindy this weekend. Heather's parent's will be there too. Can you be at our house around six on Sunday?"

"Sure."

Hanging up, Cade wondered what it could possibly be that they needed Cindy and him over for dinner.

"What was that about?" Cindy asked.

"Apparently, we are having dinner with Heather and Tommy's parents this weekend."

He was ok with it, but also wondering what they could possibly need. He instantly felt a stab of worry streak across his chest. Maybe something was wrong with Cynthia. He shook his head and figured they would have called him if there was anything like that wrong.

That weekend, they made their way to Tommy's parent's house. Once there, Cindy scooped up Cynthia and sat down her and a warm bottle of milk. Humming, she lightly tapped on Cynthia's bottom as she swayed back and forth. Cynthia fell fast asleep for Cindy and Mr. and Mrs. Lane just looked at each other, both with bags under their eyes and stains on their shirts. As Cindy swayed with Cynthia Mrs. Lane approached Cade and pulled him in close.

"We love Cynthia," she whispered with tears in her eyes. "But we wanted to know if you two were interested in adopting her?"

"What?" Cade couldn't believe they were asking this.

"Part of Tommy and Heather's will and wishes for you guys as god parents, was to adopt Cynthia if we saw that it was too much to handle in our old age. Well, we are definitely struggling."

Tommy's mom looked to pained to be asking such a thing.

"We will need to talk about it," Cade hesitated.

"We will do it," Cindy called out, overhearing the conversation.

Cade's head shot over at Cindy.

"We will?" He said.

"Why not?" Cindy shrugged. "We want a baby, we seem to be having some trouble, why not adopt her?"

Cade smiled and shook his head. He looked back to Mrs. Lane.

"Let's adopt her then."

***

Everything moved slowly within the adoption process. The state evaluated all three of them for physical or mental problems that would make them unfit for parenting or moving into a new home. Finding them both fit and healthy, and after approving their condo, Cade and Cindy got to work signing the paperwork that would make little Cynthia their own.

Even after signing all the paper work, weeks passed before a decision was made. Cade was working on a customer's tattoo, Cynthia on his mind, when his phone buzzed to life. Before he could even say 'Hello' Cindy's voice burst from the speaker.

"Cade, the adoption agency called and gave us a date!"

Hearing the excitement in her voice warmed him.

"Also, I have other news for when you get home tonight."

"Okay, I love you and I can't wait to adopt our girl."

He hung up and looked back at his customer's new tattoo.

"Sorry about that," Cade apologized. "Let's get your cleaned up."

He cleaned and wiped the area, and the customer stood to leave. Not even a moment later, another customer was sitting in his chair and he was looking over the design he had crafted for her a week ago. The process repeated through the day and Cade used his work to keep the excitement at bay.

Exhausted, he made his way home that night and found Cindy asleep on the couch with baby Cynthia in her bassinet nearby also snoring. He smiled and kissed her gently to wake her.

"Hey beautiful," he whispered.

"Hey." She stretched and looked up at him.

"Are you hungry?" He waved bags of takeout in front of her.

"Mmm, that smells delicious."

As they ate their noodles and chicken, Cade began to wonder what her other surprise was.

"So, what's going on love?" He asked. "You said you had news for me tonight?"

Cade looked at Cindy who had a large clump of noodles on the end of her chopsticks, ready to pack into her mouth. It was a comical image and he tried not to laugh, until he saw how serious her expression was.

"What's wrong?" His voice was much deeper with concern laced through it.

"Well," she looked at the fingers that rested in her lap. "You're going to be a daddy."

"I know," he stated with confusion. "Cynthia will be my little girl. We are practically blood."

He saw her shake her head and she pulled something out from behind her back. Looking down at her hand, a pregnancy test was stretched out before him. Two little lines indicating a positive test were all he needed to pull Cindy against him in a warm embrace. He kissed her shoulder as he held her close.

18

Cindy's belly grew seemingly in pace with Cynthia over the months. Cade continued to fall more and more in love with both of his girls. When he could feel the little thumps of the baby kicking and twisting inside, he was overcome with joy. He rested his head against her belly so he could listen. Soft thumps hit his cheek.

"What is he doing in there?" Cade smiled at her.

"Probably bouncing around from the ice cream."

Her eyes were cast down, and he tilted her chin up.

"Something wrong beautiful?"

"Am I?" She asked.

"Are you what?"

"Still beautiful?" Her cheeks burned with blush and he kissed her gently.

"You are always beautiful. If anything, you are even more beautiful now. I may be an artist, but I will never be able to create a masterpiece like the one in your belly."

Her smile filled him with joy.

When they made love, they had to account for the growing belly and be creative. It seemed that time just kept slipping past them. One night, when Cindy was around thirty-six weeks, she felt terrible pain in her stomach and tried to drink water, lay on her side, and use the restroom. Nothing seemed to help and the pain continued. When her pain doubled and she was seeing spots, they raced out of the condo with little Cynthia and to the hospital. Cade called Cindy's mom and she was there in no time. She kept baby Cynthia with her in the lobby as Cade went into the back with Cindy for her evaluation. Her pain had not decreased and the doctors were concerned but didn't say anything to them.

After hours of pain, they finally wheeled her back and prepped her for an emergency caesarian. Cade watched as they pulled their baby from his wife's body and took him to the warmer. His little body was quiet as they worked and he feared they might have lost him. He did not want to have to tell Cindy they had lost their beautiful baby, when he suddenly heard a cry come from the corner. Their beautiful baby boy was just fine.

"How is he?" Cindy's voice was weak and exhausted.

"He looks good," Cade responded with a relieved smile.

They had to finish closing Cindy up before they could give her their baby. When they were finally back in their own room and he rested soundly under the warmer. Cade watched her and the little guy that slept nearby. He couldn't believe he was a daddy, again, and that he had married the love of his life. He was truly happy for the first time in a long as he could remember. He walked over to their sleeping baby and placed his finger in his tiny hand, just as he had Cynthia. Caleb squeezed his father's finger tight and reassuringly. Cade promised the small little body that snoozed before him, that he would always be here for him.

"Cade?" Cindy had been sleeping so peacefully, but she was now stirring.

"I am right here, I am just holding our perfect little man's hand."

Her smile touched her eyes and he walked over to kiss her on her forehead.

"Did you ever smoke again?"

That's a random question, he thought.

"No, I guess I have just been too busy to care."
He shrugged and listened to the sounds in the hospital
room.

"Cade, I love you."

"I love you too Cindy."

Cade watched his beautiful wife fall back to sleep
and looking between her and their baby he felt a peace
come over him, but he needed one last piece to complete
the puzzle. He kissed her hand and walked out the room
to go collect their little Cynthia.